About the author

Jake Ridge is the pseudonym of Colin R Parsons. He's a fiction author who writes in many genres, such as: fantasy, sci-fi, supernatural and steampunk. He lives with his wife, Janice, in the Rhondda Valley in South Wales, UK. He's been writing for over two decades and has lots of books published for children and adults. He loves his job as an author and couldn't think of anything else he'd rather do.

By the same author

Phantom Thief & Strange Happenings

Killian Spooks Mysteries: Spirit Jumper

Jake Ridge

Killian Spooks Mysteries:
Spirit Jumper

Pegasus

A CIP catalogue record for this title is
available from the British Library

ISBN-978 1 910903 59 9

*Pegasus is an imprint of
Pegasus Elliot MacKenzie Publishers Ltd.*
www.pegasuspublishers.com

First Published in 2021

**Pegasus
Sheraton House Castle Park
Cambridge CB3 0AX England**

Printed & Bound in Great Britain

Dedication

I dedicate this book to Glyn and Mandy

Acknowledgements

Anthony Brooks for giving me the initial idea. And also, my wife, Janice, for being my sounding-board. Glyn and Mandy Davies for their continued support and for letting me use their lovely house for the setting of the story.

Chapter 1
Dead Drunk

Toady left the Square Inn and stumbled along the uneven, gravel ground. He was chuckling to himself about what his mate Robby had said to him moments earlier. He blindly stepped into a shallow hole in the tarmac and his ankle twisted, setting him off balance. He fell forward and slammed himself against the side of a car with a dull thud. It almost knocked the wind right out of him and he gasped for air for a few seconds.

'Bastering, fuck,' he cursed as he tried to push himself into a standing position. He fumbled in his pocket for his keys and realised he still held half a can of beer in his other hand. He grinned through half-open eyes and emptied the container in three gulps. Once he'd finished, he threw it to one side and began muttering. He fished in his pocket again and felt the bluntness of the key ring. He fumbled with it until he could truly grasp the troublesome fob.

It was difficult enough to hold his body upright, never mind the task of finding the right key to slip into the lock. The key wouldn't fit and he was befuddled in his stupor as to why, until he realised that it wasn't actually his car. He closed his eyes and opened his mouth and exploded a large burp, which brought on a long-winded, smelly fart.

'Aaaahh.' He expelled his relief and scolded himself for picking the wrong vehicle. 'Stupid basssaa,' he murmured. It was late and he was drunk yet again—the fourth night in a row. He twisted around from the car door and leant against it with his back. He took a deep breath through his nose and breathed out again. He looked around the car park. It was empty, but the pub was still in full swing. He could see the bright lights from the bar in the background. The chatter from his drinking pals boomed from the open windows, echoing through the summer air. Toady deliberated for a moment on whether he should go back in and have just one more drink. He wobbled slightly and thought better of it.

'Ah fuck it,' he slurred and sleepily took in another deep breath. The night air was warm with just a hint of a breeze. Toady loved this time of year and hated cold, long winters. 'See woss on the telly-when I get in,' he rambled, 'maybe drop by the Good Cod and grab some chips.' Drunkenly, he pushed himself away from the car and ambled across the car park. His trainers crunched on the broken glass of many a discarded beer bottle. It was dark where he'd left his car and he remembered why he'd parked it there. The main car park was partially lit, but he knew he was going to drink-drive so he didn't want to cause any attention to himself from the local police. If he parked around the back, he could always slip away through the lane unnoticed. He continued to try and select the right key for the door.

'Fuckin' keys,' he growled when they fell from his grasp and landed with a tinkle on the coarse ground. 'Oh shit,' he snarled and he stooped down to retrieve them. When he stood back up, he felt dizzy and he could smell his own rank breath and almost threw up there and then. He suddenly realised that he needed a piss now, too. He gave a huff of disapproval and shoved the keys back in his pocket. Toady staggered to the bushes and pushed his way through the clingy branches. 'Get-off-me-you fuckmphh,' he garbled, as thorns tore into his tee-shirt and clawed at his arms. He didn't feel the scrapes on his bare skin, but he knew it would come back with a vengeance in the morning.

It was dense darkness inside the bushes and stank of urine, which made him feel sick again. He could feel the hot bile build up in the back of his throat but managed to hold it back. He heaved a couple of times, but it eventually settled. He made doubly sure that he was hidden before he unzipped his jeans. He closed his eyes and began to relieve himself on the foliage. The feeling of release was utter heaven and even with eyes shut he had a broad smile on his face. It was worth all the hassle and fight just for that moment. Midway through his flow he had to stop, abruptly. A white light burst out of nowhere and blinded him so much that he pissed all over the legs of his trousers.

'Sh-i-t,' he slurred through gritted teeth, half in a stupor, dizzy from the sudden awakening. It caught him off guard and he toppled over. He thought he'd been caught by the police, and quickly zipped up his jeans. 'Officer, I felt ill for a second and needed to be sick.' Toady spoke to the light, not knowing who was really there. He didn't get a response from any police officer. That was weird, he thought. Then he realised that the light wasn't from a police car because there wasn't the intermittent blue flashing; it was more like a white spotlight. 'Hey, who's-ere?' Toady called out, the anger building. 'You perv?' he growled through gritted teeth.

Suddenly a whipping wind came out of nowhere and fanned the bushes around him. Beer cans and cardboard cartons flew through the air. The bushes bent back as if bowing to the light and Toady felt his hair blast from his face. He held his right hand out to shade his eyes from the bleached, white beam. But it was too blinding and windy with the dust from the car park, to make anything out.

As quickly as it flared up… it dimmed and he was left on the ground in complete darkness once more. He blinked open his eyes, not sure what had just happened. 'Wha-the-fu-wazza?' He clambered to his feet, his head swimming. The lights from the street seemed to spin like a roulette wheel. Scared, he backed out of the bush as quickly as he could, not caring what was in his way. His right foot got trapped in a twisted vine and he fell to the ground, landing on his back, on a patch of damp soil. He could feel the moisture seep through the material of his clothes; he was a mess. 'Hey-st-op-fuckin'-about-and-come-out,' he garbled, his eyes now fully open and the words barely making it from his lips. 'Come-on, I'll smash you, you fucker,' he growled.

He stopped ranting for a moment when he smelt a weird odour, which filled the air. It made him heave and this time he hurled vomit from his mouth like a fountain. Once it had finished pumping out of him, he sat up. There was a puddle of mess on the ground and some of the vomit was stuck in his hair. He wiped the excess from his mouth with the back of his hand.

There was something, or someone, moving towards him. It was too dark to make anything out. Toady leaned in to take a better look, but with his eyes blurred with tears it was impossible to focus.

'Wh-who are you?' Toady asked, his head a little clearer now, but the figure didn't answer. 'Stay there. Don't come any closer. The cops are coming,' he lied, but whatever it was, it kept on coming. Soon it was close enough to touch him. It wasn't standing on the ground. It was hovering over his body.

'Who are you? Stay away from muuaaaargh…' Toady tried to shout with mouth wide open but felt something strange enter his throat. He didn't have time to retaliate as the black substance forced its way down his windpipe. It splayed its fingers into his body like a controlled plume of never-ending smoke. Toady didn't remember any more after that; his mind went completely blank and his eyes darkened.

'You are mine now.' The gravelled voice cut through the blackness. The drunk didn't or couldn't answer. Toady's body lifted from his sitting position and stood bolt upright, like a mannequin, his green eyes, now blood red and fixed straight ahead. This wasn't Toady any more. This was a completely different being. It moved awkwardly, unused to its new form. 'What is this?' it said as the creature wobbled.

Toady's body made its way out of the car park,

leaving his car and personality behind. The host found it difficult to control this vessel. It was all loose and rubbery and was difficult to manoeuvre. The entity within scanned from side to side through Toady's eyes and made its way along the pavement. It didn't make a sound as it moved, not even a breath. All that could be heard was the swish of Toady's clothes and the light tap of his rubber trainers on concrete paving slabs. The strange being stopped and lifted its nose to sniff at the air; its blotchy, red eyes followed the direction of the nose. It needed a fresher body, one that wasn't as intoxicated and as unfit as this one. It would have to search around this new place until it found something.

Toady's cumbersome walk along the pathway didn't catch anyone's attention. This was mainly because he was drunk most of the time anyway and that's how he normally ambled down the high street. There was a group of young women heading his way. Toady's head tilted back and it sniffed the air once more. Toady's face didn't show any emotion as he neared his next victims. The girls were on a pub-crawl, making their way to the next watering hole. They were shouting and screaming and laughing.

Toady stopped as they approached.

'What the fuck are you looking at you perv,' one girl rasped. 'Yuck, this guy is staring at me,' she complained.

'Yeah, fuck off,' came the voice of another. Toady stepped forward and grabbed the nearest woman by the hair and yanked her head back. And then, before she or her friends had a chance to stop him, Toady clamped his mouth over hers, in a forced, disgusting, kiss.

'Hey, get off her you prick,' one of her friends screamed, but it was too late. The victim didn't even have a chance to scream. She tried to kick and pull away, but the creature was too strong.

And that was when the host crawled out of Toady's body and made its way into the new vessel. The girl's other friends tried to pull Toady off her, but after a moment he just fell lifelessly to the pavement and didn't move again.

'Julie, Julie, are you, all right?' her best friend shrieked. All around the women were in turmoil. One was already phoning the police from her mobile when Julie stood bolt upright and turned on the girls. She stuck out her hand and clamped it on her friend's face. She screamed, but the entity sucked all the life out of her in an instant, and let go. The girl—now a withered husk—dropped to the ground. There were piercing screams as the rest of them tried to flee. Julie grabbed her other friend by her ponytail, yanked her head back and locked onto her mouth, just like it had done from Toady. She sucked in another life and let her friend's body drop to the ground. The remaining three ran off, screaming and crying, one throwing up violently as she made her escape.

The creature calmly decided not to pursue them. The entity was quite satisfied with this new body. It walked more naturally from the main street towards the park. The eyes were bloodshot, but the spirit inside was getting stronger. This vessel had a pleasant smell and the torso was in much better shape. It needed to find somewhere safe to rest before the sun came up and it searched the girl's mind. All the information it needed came flooding through and the creature knew exactly where to go!

Chapter 2
Eavesdrop

Killian Spooks had only just got back from solving a particularly unusual case and was tired. He told the Uber driver to pull up, and he got out. It was getting late but he decided to drop by his favourite pub for a quick pint. He felt a buzz of excitement as he stepped inside. He ordered his usual and took his drink to the nearest table. He poured the bottle into the glass and, when it was full, placed the bottle next to it. He slouched back in the creaky, chair and took a couple of gulps of Cambrian Lite, his favourite tipple. There were two guys at the counter deep in an intense conversation. One was tall and thickset while the other was slightly shorter and thin as a straw. They were loud and excited about something. This caught Killian's attention. He hated losing out on the latest news and closed his eyes while he swallowed, listening in on their private conversation.

'Yeah, really weird. I heard it was Toady of all people, is that true?' the big guy asked. He was hunched over the countertop with his arms clasped around his pint as if guarding it. Who would be stupid enough to take it, Killian didn't know? The large man was staring straight into his mate's face. The warlock saw there was a gap between the guy's shirt and the waistband of his shorts, which revealed the worst butt crack he'd ever seen. Killian shuddered. He kept his ears pricked without appearing too obvious.

'He doesn't normally say boo to a bear,' the smaller one said. 'You only know he's there when he falls off the stool, but last night…' He dropped his voice to a whisper and his drinking buddy leaned in. 'Last night,' he repeated, 'he attacked a bunch of girls on a hen night. From what I can make out, he forced one to kiss him.' Killian arched his brow. 'Then, soon after,' the smaller man continued, 'collapsed and died, right there and then.'

'Wow, that *is* crazy,' the big guy agreed. 'He's normally too smashed to do anything. Don't sound like him, but you never know.'

'Not only that, but I heard that the girl he kissed then attacked her friends. She killed two of them and the others got away.' The smaller man eyes widened as he said the words.

'Christ, and this all happened just down the road?'

The big guy nodded. 'You can't miss the police tape and forensics tent coming through town.'

'Yeah. Toady's car was left in the car park,' the slight man said, 'and he never walks. How he hasn't been pulled in for drink driving I'll never know. Doesn't matter now though.'

'Yeah, I know. So why *was* he walking do you think? I've seen that crazy bastard drive many times, fully loaded,' the big guy said. 'He rolls along slowly down the back lane.'

'Well. Whatever. They're looking for the girl he attacked… Anyway, it's your turn for a round, Joe,' the smaller one said, and that was when Killian broke away.

This story made the wizard's eyes narrow and he began biting his bottom lip. He'd missed the crime scene. But that was because he'd come to town in a different direction. He reached for the bottle and poured the last of the contents into his glass and watched the bubbles rise in the pale, amber liquid. Killian's mind was working ten to the dozen.

'A spirit jumper,' he mumbled and took a sip. 'I haven't come across one of them in a long, long while.' He stroked the stubble on his chin thoughtfully. How did a *jumper* cross over from the other side, he pondered and scratched his head. I've got to check this out. This could be very dangerous. Killian drained the glass and placed the bottle and glass on the bar as he left, giving the landlord a nod. He walked outside into the hot, summer heat. He knew what car Toady owned and it wouldn't be too difficult to find it in the car park. It was probably a crime scene at this point.

Killian looked in the beer garden; it was filled with punters enjoying the warm weather. He liked the Square Inn pub because you could sit inside or out in complete anonymity. It was the kind of place where no one batted an eyelid unless you wanted to talk. It was always busy, too. No matter what time of day or night. Killian was an observer; he had to be in his job. He checked out all the comings and goings in the pub. He remembered when he'd been in there, that there was a guy, who always sat quietly in the corner, getting wasted. That was probably Toady. It wasn't a healthy way to live, but everyone has his or her own story. He didn't judge.

Killian had also noticed that he always parked his beaten-up Ford Focus at the back end of the car park. So he made his way there. The spot was empty — surprise-surprise — but the remains of the yellow and black crime tape marked out the area. Killian stood for a moment observing, noting that there was something unusual in the air, a faint odour emitting from the bush next to the tape. The wizard's aura was tingling — this is where it happened, he realised.

He broke from his thoughts and made his way out of the car park and along the street. There was more crime tape and a tent just down the road where the killings had taken place. There was a lonely cop standing guard. The wizard walked around the obstruction. He strolled past the shops and offices and made for home. It was ten-thirty at night and the streets were mostly deserted. A few stragglers were milling around, as he walked towards his apartment, but otherwise nothing unusual.

Glenside Printing was a company smack on the edge of the town of Windy Vale. Killian's apartment was on the top floor. He fished for his keys and unlocked the door. He then walked the corridor to the bottom of the stairs. The light was on, but there again the light was always on. He could hear the throbbing and clunking of machinery in the basement; the printing machines were in full swing. Glyn must have an urgent job on, he assumed; the owner worked into the night a lot of the time. Killian admired the guy and his wife, Mandy, salt of the earth and hard workers.

The wooden stairs creaked and groaned as he climbed to his floor. Finally, he arrived at his flat. The yellow glow from the overhead light shone on the half-glass panel. It used to be an office with a stockroom at the back. But in the last year or so, it was Killian's apartment and he loved the solitude. The building had beautifully crafted wood panelling. The smell from the printing shop below hung in the air. He didn't know why, but he loved the odour of ink and machine fluid.

Killian Spooks, besides being a wizard, was also supernatural, which meant the magical and spiritual world was his playground. He stepped inside his office and flicked on the light. The room was nothing special and he barely used it. There was a desk with a bunch of papers scattered over the surface and a landline phone. There was also a swivel chair, the leather of which had worn through to the frame in parts. A small, unassuming filing cabinet sat in the corner, covered in dust. The room itself could have done with some colour, but décor wasn't at the forefront of Killian's mind.

There was also a faded picture, which hung on the wall, depicting a bowl of fruit. It was ironic because Killian didn't eat fruit. The frame had seen better days too and so had the room, if he was honest. He walked through to his apartment, which was as drab as the office. When he'd moved in he left things, more or less, just as they were. Inside, lay a sofa and a small coffee table, which was situated in the middle of the room. On the wall, there were some fitted shelves filled with scrolls and books — his magical and spiritual world of information. He threw his keys on the table and walked over to the bookcase. He peered at the dusty, book spines. These very books had helped him solve many cases over the years.

Killian was a tall man with brown wavy hair, which hadn't been cut or groomed. He often didn't shave for days, which either left him with a thickening beard or heavy stubble. His green eyes were almost translucent and brightened up his scruffy appearance. Even being so tall, he was an unassuming character. He always wore brown canvas trousers and tan boots topped off with a beige tee-shirt, but occasionally wore blue when he was feeling adventurous. He also wore a jacket with lots of pockets to keep his work stuff when he was on a case.

'Spirit Jumper,' he whispered to himself while running his index finger along a line of books. He dropped down to the second row and continued along the spines. 'Ah-ha,' he said, his green eyes flashing with excitement. He selected the title he was searching for: *Movement of the Paranormal World*. He sat on the sofa and placed the large book on the coffee table, dust rising in a small cloud. He traced his finger down the pages and flipped over again and again until he came across the page, he was interested in.

'Entities can inhabit a living body as long as they need to use it. They will then move on to the next vessel at will. But will only stay if the vessel is sound and healthy. If a body is deceased, the essence of the spirit can't penetrate the dead vessel.

Interesting,' Killian said and read on. '*So it can't hide in the morgue. Once a spirit inhabits a host it likes, it can make that person do as it pleases and no one would know any different. It also has to draw the life force from other bodies to keep it fresh.*'

Killian looked away from the page and stared in thought. '*The entity is at its weakest in direct daylight. This is the best time to strike and send the demon spirit back to whence it came.*'

Killian was puzzled. What was a spirit jumper doing here, in his town? There must be a reason? Someone had called it here? He snapped away from his thoughts when the phone rang.

'Wow, that doesn't happen very often,' he said. He got up off the sofa and quickly went into his office. He grabbed the Bakelite phone.

'Good evening, am I speaking to Mr Killian Spooks?' the voice asked. It had a slight military edge to it.

'Yes, speaking, who is this?' Killian probed, intrigued.

'I am Chief Inspector Daniel Hathaway. I need your, er, services,' he said, not sounding convinced at what he was asking.

'I take it you don't approve of my profession, Mr Hathaway?' Killian spoke directly, picking up on the vibe of the conversation. He stared at the basket of fruit on the wall. People just didn't believe, or want to believe, that what he was doing

27

was of value. He'd been called a fake and a liar on many occasions, more than he could remember.

'What I approve of, and what I have to deal with, are two very different things, Mr Spooks,' Hathaway rasped. Killian could feel his body stiffen in temper and pulled the receiver away from his ear. He rested it on his chest. He could still hear the inspector's voice, blustering through the speaker.

'Mr Spooks, Mr Spooks,' he ranted. Killian took a deep breath and lifted the phone to his mouth.

'What can I do for you, Chief Inspector?' Killian said with a lighter tone.

'Ah, there you are, I lost you for a moment. I've been advised that you can, er, deal with certain… weird situations?' he continued.

'I can, and have done for several years,' Killian responded.

'Well, I need help with this, um, a personality change situation that's plaguing the city,' he stated. 'My officers have enough to do without having this to solve as well.'

'Okay,' Killian said.

'Well, can you help?' the chief responded abruptly.

'I can investigate, but there is a fee and no guarantees,' Killian said, 'and I'll need your utmost cooperation,' he added, eyes narrowing.

'That won't be a problem. You will have a free run at doing… whatever it is that you do. But please try and get me something I can work with,' the chief said.

'Can you send me all the information you have on this case?' the wizard asked.

'Yes, give me your email,' the inspector asked.

'I don't do email,' Killian replied. 'Me and tech don't get along.'

'Don't do emails, that's absurd,' the inspector muttered incredulously. 'Okay then, I can have it sent to your address,' he continued.

Killian relayed his address back to the inspector. 'I charge by the day.' Killian said.

'Yes, yes, I can get one of my staff to deal with your finances,' Hathaway said, sounding reluctant to talk about money.

'I'll start on this as soon as I get your paperwork. Oh, by the way, Chief Inspector, who told you about me?' Killian probed.

'One of my colleagues came across an advert you put in the local paper, I think. Don't get me wrong, Spooks, I want results ASAP and if I'm happy with what you come up with, well, who knows, it could lead to other cases,' the chief inspector added.

'I'll need some money to start the investigation,' Killian said, and waited.

'How much are we talking?' the chief

responded.

'Two grand should do it,' Killian said smoothly, eagerly waiting for the response but trying not to sound too excited.

'What? Er… oh, all right, give me your details and I'll make sure you get the money you require transferred to your account. Get me some results, Spooks,' he said, his tone acid, and he slammed the phone down.

'Charming,' Killian said and gave a wry smile. 'More cases, eh?' Killian rubbed the earpiece on his stubbly chin. 'There must be a lot of stuff the police can't deal with in this town.' The wizard smiled and placed the phone in the cradle. Before he went off to bed, he took more of his books from his bookcase. This wasn't going to be an easy job.

Chapter 3
Penny White

Killian woke the following morning to the sounds of banging on his office door. He gave a squint at the clock—it was nine-fifteen. He grunted as he rolled over onto his back.

Who the fuck was banging his door at this time of the morning? He closed his eyes and took a deep intake of breath. How did they get to his office, he pondered. The downstairs door should have been locked... *ah!* Then he remembered that Glyn's wife, Mandy, always unlocked the door downstairs really early for deliveries. He sat up and swung his legs over the side of the bed. It was warm already and the room was stuffy. Killian pulled back the curtains and the sun threw a long solid glow on the mat. He lifted the handle and pushed open the panel. The cool air rushed in and washed over him like a shower. He stood for a moment listening to the sounds of everyday life below. The grating noise continued to pound his head. It was that irritatingly tinny sound of metal against glass. Maybe rings on the caller's fingers. He wandered into his office in a half-stupor, dressed only in a pair of boxer shorts. He stared at the glass panel in the door. He could just make out the shape of a figure through the frosted pane.

'All right, all right, I'm coming, I'm coming. Stop with the banging, for God's sake,' he yelled.

A soft voice emanated from beyond the office. 'I'm Penny White, Mr Spooks, from police headquarters. Chief Inspector Daniel Hathaway sent me. I have some paperwork for you,' the female said, sounding irritated but very professional.

'Okay,' Killian relented and then remembered the conversation he'd had on the phone the night before. The chief inspector did say he'd send someone round with some information regarding the strange happenings. Killian reached out and clicked the lock. The door swung open freely. Killian wasn't prepared for what would happen next… he stopped dead in his tracks. There was the most attractive woman he'd ever laid eyes on. She was of medium height, with a slender frame, long, black hair tied in a ponytail. Her lips were full, rich scarlet and her eyes mesmerising, the deepest blue. He instantly noticed that the top two buttons of her cream blouse were undone, revealing her slim neck and a hint of a plunging cleavage. The fine, gold necklace she wore complemented her smooth, olive skin. She didn't wear heels, but black wedges and tight-fitting grey skirt—very official. He felt himself staring and brought his gaze up to her eyes. He caught her looking at his attire and she quickly aligned her eyes back with his.

'Are you all right, Mr Spooks? You look a little vacant,' she said.

'I've just woken up because someone was banging on my door at this early hour,' he complained.

'I do apologise for waking you up, Mr Spooks,' she continued, 'but these are normal office hours. It's hardly early in the morning is it?' Penny countered.

'Well, you're annoying,' Killian rasped.

'You're not exactly sociable either.' She glared at him with her bright, blue globes. He looked down to her waist and the file she was clutching with both hands. He noticed that she wasn't wearing a wedding ring. But he observed that on her right-hand she had a gold ring on her third finger. That's what had made the excruciating sound on the glass. So she wasn't married. Not that it mattered these days, but she looked the type of person who had a certain order to her life. Perhaps she had a boyfriend or girlfriend. It didn't concern him at that point because she was irritating the hell out of him.

Killian stood there half-naked with his hair the same as the day before and thick stubble on his chin. Penny White, in contrast, looked immaculate. To say he felt a bit awkward in his undies was an understatement. Suddenly, they stopped talking and there was a pause that was only broken by the distant chugging of the machinery below. He sucked in heavily through his nose and calmed.

'Is that for me?' he asked, pointing at the folder. He could see her face relax and her glare soften.

'I've been told to, um… give you any help that you need, Mr Spooks,' she said reluctantly, but also trying to remain professional. Killian could tell from her tone that she didn't want to do it. 'Chief Inspector Hathaway was very insistent that I-I…' she stumbled. Was she intimidated by his ravishingly good looks? He smiled. 'What are you smiling at, Mr Spooks?' she demanded, her eyes narrowed and her nose flared. He couldn't help it. She looked really cute when she was annoyed.

'Nothing in particular,' he said. 'I won't need any help at all. That won't be necessary—I work alone, Miss White,' Killian said and reached out his hand to grab the file. This realisation seemed to calm her and her face relaxed. Killian was drinking in her sweet intoxicating perfume—it made him feel giddy. He snapped out of it. He was a professional too, damn it!

'We're paying you a fair amount of money, Mr Spooks, so please keep us updated,' she said abruptly.

'Really? I'm pretty sure you aren't paying me anything out of your pocket, Miss White. All you have to do is receive my reports and sign the cheques... after they've been authorised by your boss, of course,' Killian retorted, peering deep into her eyes.

She countered quickly. 'Is that really your name, Mr Spooks?' she questioned. 'Or have you only used it for your professional needs?' Sarcasm underlined her words. Her face gave away a look of satisfaction.

'What, Spooks?' Killian answered, but not giving anything away, and annoyed at the questions this office clerk was firing at him.

'Yes, well, you're a psychic, ghost hunter or something, aren't you? I've seen it on the telly. Is it a made-up name for your profession?' she asked, and it sounded both patronising and offensive.

He glared at her. 'Yes, yes, it is actually my birth name,' he snapped. 'I come from a long line of Spooks. It's been in my family for hundreds of years. So you assumed that I'd made it up, did you? The spooky Mr Spooks,' Killian chided and made hand gestures by wiggling his fingers in a ghostly way. He could tell she was embarrassed and didn't know how to respond. 'Do you treat all your business associates in this way, Miss White?' Killian demanded. He was enjoying making her squirm. Her powder-white make-up suddenly turned a shade of crimson and she shifted awkwardly in her stance. Killian was now beginning to feel uncomfortable for making her feel insecure.

'I'm er, sorry, Mr Spooks. That wasn't my intention and that was very unprofessional of me,' she apologised, realising that she'd gone too far. 'Please feel free to report me to my superiors for any misconduct.' She very skilfully tucked the file under her arm and snapped open her shoulder bag. Killian was taken aback as she dug into her purse and produced her cards. 'Here's my full name and I.D. I do apologise again, Mr Spooks.'

Killian softened right away. He could see she was in a state. Her hair was pristine as it was tied back when she'd first arrived. Now loose strands had escaped the hair-band and draped over her face, making her look even hotter, if Killian was truthful with himself.

'What? No, I'm not reporting you to anybody, Miss White,' Killian confessed and had by then, calmed somewhat. 'I suppose it does sound strange, with me being a wizard and all,' he smiled. 'I do get strange looks from people when I mention that.'

Penny placed the card back in her purse. 'You're a *wizard*?' She managed to return a sweet grin and he loved how the corners of her mouth curled up when she was happy. 'What, a real wizard like — '

'Please, please,' he cut in sharply, 'don't say what I think you're going to say. Not the boy wizard thing. That is the first thing everybody says to me and it drives me up the wall.'

'Oh. I don't want to make things any more weird, between us, I mean in our professional relationship,' she corrected. 'I... withdraw that last remark.'

He chuckled. 'You sound like a lawyer, Miss White.'

She burst out with a chuckle too and it made her lurch forward.

'And yes, I am a wizard, warlock or sorcerer, whatever you want to call it,' he said, and looked at her with bemusement. 'Look, let's start again, shall we?' Killian continued and looked at her warmly. 'None of this conversation has gone the way I wanted it to go.'

'Okay,' Penny agreed with a nod. 'I can do that.'

'I'm Killian Spooks, very pleased to meet you,' he said politely.

'Penny White, likewise, I'm sure,' she responded.

'So, you have that file for me, I take it?' he said, looking at the folder she was holding.

'Yes,' she said and handed it to him. 'All

progress reports need to be sent directly to me,' she said, without breaking eye contact. 'Chief Inspector Hathaway's explicit instructions, and believe me he's a stickler.'

Killian loved it when she got *all-official* because her nose wrinkled and a cute, crooked line appeared on her forehead. He smiled again and she didn't know how to take it but said nothing.

'Yes, he sounded very official on the phone last night,' Killian remembered.

'It's his way. He's very methodical,' she said and continued with that smile.

'Well, when I have something, you'll be the first to know, Miss White — I'll be in touch,' Killian said, holding the file in his hand, and suddenly felt the breeze from the corridor blow, up his shorts. She looked at him as he gave a sudden shiver.

'I'll let you get dressed,' she said, looking at his attire.

He looked down at the dishevelled appearance and lifted his gaze back to her again. 'You caught me at a bad time,' he joked. 'I'm normally a lot more organised than this,' he said, not even believing his own statement.

'Here's my personal number,' she said, 'to contact me if you've got something important and it's after hours.' Penny handed him her official business card. So, was she in a relationship? Well, she was offering her number—this pleased Killian.

'Okay, I thank you,' Killian responded, as he took it from her. 'I will keep you informed, Miss White,' he said, and with that, there was a few seconds pause—just the two of them looking at one another and not talking. The dreamy eye contact seemed to go on for a while, until Penny blinked. She caught what she was doing and so did Killian, for his part. They broke away and he cleared his throat.

'Please, call me Penny,' she said softly and added that perfect smile again.

'Oh, okay,' Killian agreed. 'Instead of Mr Spooks you could call me Killian,' he added.

'Well, okay,' she nodded. 'Bye, Killian.'

'Goodbye, Penny,' Killian said as Penny turned away and walked slowly along the corridor. From Killian's point of view, she seemed to glide. He deliberately watched her butt move from side-to-side as she disappeared down the stairs. She smiled to herself, knowing he was still looking in her direction. Killian pushed the door shut behind him and leaned back against it. Wow, he thought, he could not believe what just happened and let out a chuckle. Wow, she is gorgeous,' he thought. He held that in his mind and stayed put for a few seconds more and eventually snapped out of it.

He walked back inside his room and made a

coffee and a couple of slices of toast. He then laid the file open on the coffee table. He skimmed through it, trying not to get any grease from the butter onto the pages. After he'd pored over it and taken in the details, he finished up and put the folder away. He threw the washing up into the sink and then took a really long shower, thinking of Miss Penny White…

Chapter 4
The White House

The information in the file took Killian to Seventy-Seven Oak Drive and Miss Stella Winter's house. He didn't expect Stella to be there, especially as the police had already been the night before. But what he did know was that the spirit inside her would tend to find her family. Once that was established, then either it could inhabit them one by one, or just relieve them of their life force by killing them all off in one big massacre. Killian didn't much relish the latter, but it was inevitable in his line of work. Spirits, demons, ghouls, bogarts and all the rest were very unpredictable.

Killian rattled up on his Vespa and parked it in a layby next to the bushes. He took off his helmet and placed it on top of the seat. He strolled towards the housing estate and gave a glance back at his powder blue scooter before he continued. He grinned a little smile of approval — not many wizards owned one of those, he thought. It was his pride and joy. Killian didn't want a big muscle car or a family saloon — his little motorbike was perfect. He mumbled something under his breath and the scooter disappeared from view. Melted into the background. If they can't see it, they won't be able to steal it, he thought.

It was lunchtime and the area was mostly empty except for a keen gardener who was mowing his lawn. There was a woman — Killian assumed she was the guy's wife — pruning something or other at the border of the property. Killian wasn't interested in the fundamentals — he hated gardening with a vengeance. He didn't mind sitting in Glyn's garden out back because he knew he didn't have to maintain it.

Killian walked along the pavement as unassumingly as he could. It was hot, the middle of June. The sun was high and the heady odour of grass clippings forced its way up his nostrils. His jacket was a mistake in this heat, but he kept all his *instruments* in the pockets, so he had no choice. He stopped and felt something, a tingle to his wizard senses. There was a power at work here, or had been. He hadn't been quite sure. That confirmed it and he knew he was on the right track. Killian was focused as he walked along the pavement.

The sorcerer looked into the distance and made out a big, white house set in a cul-de-sac. There were three cars parked outside. It was a lovely spot with a mass of fir trees keeping the property hidden. Alarm bells rang as soon as

Killian Spooks saw the vehicles, though. It was gone noon, so why would there be a full complement of cars outside? Didn't anyone work over there? This wasn't good. He could feel his heart quicken, and a layer of sweat on his lip and leaking down his forehead.

Killian strolled warily up the path to the front of the house. The big, white door was slightly open and this made his stomach tighten. His senses were now tingling like crazy. He knew he had to go in there, but at times like these he wished he had someone else with him. Just because he was a wizard didn't make him invincible.

Killian gently pushed the door and it swung open silently. The sun spilled inside making an awkward yellow shape on the floor, the floor was barely visible. Everything was completely quiet. There wasn't even the sound of a ticking clock. His hands were clammy and began to shake. He clamped them into fists to reassure himself. His breathing came in fits and starts. He ran his tongue over his lips and swallowed down the saliva. It's the middle of the day, he told himself.

'Spirits are at their weakest in the day,' he mumbled, but that didn't calm his nerves, although it did give him a modicum of courage. He was about to call out but his voice was strained and came out all husky and thin. He cleared his throat and tried again.

'Miss Stella Winter,' Killian called out, really hoping she wouldn't appear. His voice trailed off into the vast hallway. He noticed that everything in there was white. The walls, ceiling, even down to the floor tiles. He spied a winding staircase to his right and yes, that was brilliant, white too. But there was no sign of anyone at all, and that was absurd considering the vehicles in the driveway. Where was everyone? Where were they indeed?

'Miss Stella Winter,' he shouted this time, but nothing came back. He had to go in further and this made him grind his teeth. It was pointless calling the cops because if it was just his senses mixed up, then Chief Inspector Hathaway would have a field day and never hire him again. He breathed hard then moved on. There were three doors to choose from—one to the right of the staircase, and two more to the left. One of them he assumed would lead to the living room and he thought maybe the other would lead to the kitchen. 'Living room, it is,' he said, finding his throat dry from the air-con.

He looked at the glossy, white door and could feel his hands almost sparking with electrical energy. Killian's breathing became rapid. He dipped into his pocket and pulled out a silver pen and a sense of calmness warmed him. It wasn't just a writing instrument, but in fact, it was Killian's wand. Not what anyone would expect, but it had helped him out of many a situation and he needed anything he could get right now. He held it up in his right hand and reached out to twist the doorknob with his left; it clicked, which made his stomach flip.

'Calm down, Killian,' he hissed. The wand was warm in his hand and made his palms clammy. His breathing came in short blasts.

He tentatively stepped through into the unknown. Once inside he saw that the room was light and airy. White everywhere as in the foyer: curtains, ceiling, walls, sofa and even floorboards.

'Way too much white, man,' he whispered. He clocked the rug that lay in front of the sofa right away—it was charcoal black. It was such a huge contrast to the rest of the house. This was what Killian was expecting. He walked closer to it to get a better look. There were two charred body shapes embedded in the fibres with some of the dust particles spilled onto the wooden floor. Killian looked on and realised that these two mangled figures must be Stella's parents. Their life forces sucked completely from their bodies. Killian winced. How terrified they must have been before they died. This must have happened after the police had searched the property, he assumed.

He raised the wand and heard the crackle of energy surge through it. So, was the entity still in there? Killian's face tightened and his eyes were at their widest. He methodically searched each room of the rest of the house. There was nothing – the entity was long gone. He put his magical pen back in his pocket and leaned against the door pillar leading into the living room.

'Where the hell would it go?' he puzzled. 'Well let's look at the facts,' he said out loud and stroked his cheeks. 'It's inhabiting a body that the police are already looking for, so it needs to swap sooner rather than later. How do I find it? Of course,' he said with a burst of excitement. The answer was staring him right in the face. The bodies that were decomposed in the living room – he needed to syphon the spirit's essence or DNA while it was still fresh.

He knelt and grabbed a penknife from another pocket. He also pulled out a small plastic bag. He winced as he scraped some of the charcoal substance straight into the transparent pocket and quickly sealed it. The smell was horrendous. He felt sick and had to get out of there. He could never get used to the smell of decomposed bodies, but when they'd been absorbed by a spirit it was even worse. He knew what he had to do now, and that was to put the contents of the bag into his "essence finder". But the gadget he needed was in the compartment of his scooter.

The other problem Killian had, was time. He knew he had to call the cops and tell them about the bodies and that would be an awkward conversation. Even though he was working for the chief now, he would still be detained for ages and didn't have time for all that questioning. So he did the next best thing and called the police from the landline in the kitchen, but didn't give a name and disguised his voice. Most people didn't know that once you ring the cops, they could keep your line open, until they were satisfied that you're not involved in the crime you're reporting.

He didn't want to tie-up his phone, which was the only technology he owned. He quickly grabbed his wand again and did a sweep of his own to dissolve his DNA. He also used a spell to magically remove his image from the camera footage so that it appeared that he'd not even set foot in there. Once that was done, he moved stealthily out of the street, avoiding Mr and Mrs Serious Gardener on the way to his scooter.

Luckily for him the layby was hidden from view by high hedges, so when the police arrived, they wouldn't see him. Killian quickly removed the cloaking spell and flipped open his seat, unlocking the compartment he'd had specially made. The essence finder was a wooden box about the size of a cigarette packet. It didn't look like anything special, just a wooden box. But when laid flat it had a small, clear glass dome fixed on top and a pull-out tray on the side. Killian grabbed the plastic bag from his pocket, emptied half the contents into the tray and pushed it closed. He waited a moment and took a look around to see if anyone was watching. He soon heard police sirens in the background and wanted to get out of there as soon as possible. Soon the air would be filled with blue lights and swarms of police cars.

The glass dome began to mist up and a picture appeared in place of the grey, wispy fog. Killian peered into the glass and found that he could see through the eyes of the spirit. This was both fascinating and scary. Imagine looking through someone else's eyes. He could see — at close quarters — the person that the entity was going to inhabit in the next couple of seconds. They were kissing but, unbeknown to the new victim, it was the kiss of death. The victim probably thought that a blowjob with a beautiful, sex-starved woman was on the cards. But it didn't quite get that far. The image soon flipped around and now Killian was looking at Stella Winter on the ground, decomposing into a charcoal mound. Killian winced. This thing had to be stopped, and the sooner the better.

The wizard looked more closely at the image in the glass and could make out a sign in the darkened corridor. Shambles Shopping Centre. He now had an image of the person he was looking for and a location in which to find him. But how long would it stay in that body? And how long would it stay there in the shopping mall? The picture in the glass began to fade and soon the dome was clear again. Killian pulled out the wooden drawer; it was empty now. Its job was done. The sirens were quite loud — the police were here and Killian needed to be somewhere else. He swiftly put everything away and got his helmet. He was soon dashing along the road, heading towards the shopping precinct.

Chapter 5
Shadow Nymph

The Vespa's engine gave a rumble and then finally died. Killian parked it up around the side of the building behind a dumpster. He administered his usual spell so that he could hide it. He stood quietly for a moment taking in the static atmosphere. Killian's senses pulled him towards the museum instead of the shopping centre. Something was definitely inside that old place. This case needed to be solved sooner than later or a lot more innocent people were going to die. The tingling in his fingers told him that the power in there was far superior to anything he'd dealt with before.

He scanned the outside of the building. There was a small car park at the front but it hadn't seen much in the way of traffic for a long while. The heat vapours were rising from the tarmac, which was cracked like a jigsaw puzzle, with grass and weeds pushing through all the gaps. Killian felt a real pang of sadness. He loved history and places like these need to be preserved and used. There was far too much distraction with video games these days. Killian snapped from his thoughts and concentrated — he had a job to do.

Time was moving on and by now it was mid-afternoon. The sun beat down, draining his strength. He felt tired and the thought of a pint right now in the Square Inn was overwhelming, but he shook it off. He looked at the museum. It was a pretty run down and in desperate need of restoration. It didn't look as though it was open and hadn't been for a long time. He shuddered and took in a mouthful of air. This was a perfect place to hold out — a disused building right next to a shopping mall. The host could pick and choose its victims and entice them back here. Killian shuddered at the thought. He needed something to protect himself with and patted his pocket with the pen. but didn't pull it out.

'Okay, let's go,' he said, as if talking to someone. At that precise moment, his phone rang out to the tune of *Spirit in the Sky*. He had to smile at the irony, every time. He grabbed it and looked at the screen — it read "Unknown Source". Killian's eyes widened. That wasn't supposed to happen. His mobile wasn't an ordinary one — it wasn't connected to the normal network. This handset was on a different frequency to terrestrial mobile phones. No one could know his number unless they were of a supernatural or of a higher power. So who was this? Killian put the phone to his ear and listened. No one spoke on the other end. Killian decided to speak.

'You've rung a private number,' he barked. 'Whoever this is, you should stop right now and hang up.' There was a pause. All Killian could hear on the line was a hiss.

'Hello, Mr Spooks.' A soft female voice spoke up. It had a youthful quality. Like someone in their early twenties or at least that, was Killian's interpretation.

'Who are you?' Killian fumed. 'And how did you get this number? This mobile is on a private frequency, so you've either stumbled on it or —'

'Why, Mr Spooks, that was the easy part,' the woman said in a velvety tone, cutting him off. 'The hard part was tracking you down.' He could hear a chuckle in her voice.

'Look, I don't know how you know my name or anything else for that matter. So I'm going to have to ring off now. I haven't got time for this. I have a very important appointment. Please, don't call this number again,' Killian said, his annoyance obvious. He was about to end the connection when...

'Fair enough,' the voice replied, but it seemed so close. It wasn't on his phone speaker any longer; it came from right behind him. Killian froze and reached in his pocket for his wand. He grabbed it in readiness and turned. He came face-to-face with a beautiful young woman. He peered at her and relaxed his grip on the wand. The girl returned the look with an added grin.

She was tall, maybe six feet. She had a near-perfect complexion, with the bluest eyes you could just dive into. Her face featured high, handsome cheekbones with a slender nose and very red lips. Her black hair spilt over her shoulders in a thick mane. She stood in a tight leather jumpsuit, which hugged every curve. And the tingle he felt told him that she was radiating a powerful force of some kind.

'Who are you, and more importantly, why are you following me? Not only that, but how did you find me?' Killian pressured her for an answer.

'I assumed you needed help,' she responded, simply beaming a wider smile.

'Help? Help with what?' he countered flippantly. 'You don't know what I'm doing here, but you do know my name.'

'I know you're a wizard and that's why your hand is hovering there... A wand, I'm guessing?' she said and Killian didn't waver. 'I also know you need to stop whatever lies inside that place,' she said, and pointed a slender finger at the museum. Killian was more than agitated.

'How and why do you know about any of this?' Killian was very cautious. Why would this person come to a run-down museum, he thought.

'I don't need help with anything. Now go away,' he insisted.

'I'm guessing that it'll take the two of us to sort out that little problem,' she said, and with that Killian was at a loss. He didn't like this. He didn't like this at all. She knew everything he knew and that was bad enough. He didn't know anything about her, except the fact that she was immortal.

'Okay, that's it. Who are you?' Killian demanded. 'Spit it out.' And with that, he dipped into his pocket and produced the wand. He pointed it at her; it crackled into life and she flinched.

'How very uncouth, Mr Spooks. I am Cleo Smoke. You won't need to use that on me,' she said with a cheery smile. 'I'm a –'

'Shadow nymph.' Killian said, cutting her off. 'I know what you are.' She nodded in appreciation.

'So you've worked that out?' she replied. 'Well, you are a wizard, and wizards do have a way of finding things out.'

'Cleo Smoke?' Killian said with a tight grin. 'Quaint name.'

'My *chosen* name for this world,' she replied smartly. 'Could you please put that away?' She indicated the wand. 'You wouldn't want to get too excited and set it off in your hand.' He looked at her and shook his head.

'Really, using sexual innuendo?' Killian retorted.

'A girl can have her fun, can't she?' Cleo said.

'I understand the chosen name thing, caution is everything crossing worlds,' Killian responded. (Once you've crossed over from one world to another, you never use your original name. That name is your code and it can weaken and destroy you if your secret is breached.) 'Why are you here, Cleo?' Killian lightened up on his approach and lowered his wand. 'It can't be just for my devilish charm,' he beamed, but she didn't respond to his quip and turned cold for a moment.

'That fucking thing in there, killed my best friend,' she said, her eyes serious, teeth clenched. 'It must not get away.'

Killian felt her pain. It came across so genuinely. 'Uh, I'm so sorry. I really am, Miss Smoke. Who was your friend?' Killian asked, with concern this time. He could see she was hurting.

'Stella Winter,' Cleo confessed. Killian's eyes flickered and he put the wand back in his pocket and it changed back into a pen. 'She didn't ask for any of this. And that thing tossed her aside like she meant nothing to this world,' Cleo continued, with venom bubbling under the surface. Killian breathed a shallow, long breath. He'd witnessed her death only a short while ago through his essence finder.

'Ok. I'm curious and I have to ask you this,' the wizard said, trying to calm her. 'How does a shadow nymph become friends with a mortal?' He needed to know more about her. 'Immortals and mortals don't mix in a normal situation. So how did you two cross paths?'

'I visit this world from time to time. It's lonely on the other side,' she confessed. Killian nodded his acknowledgement—he knew only too well. 'I needed a friend and Stella was there for me. She was warm, loving and kind. The friendliest person you could ever wish to meet.' Killian could see her eyes begin to fill, but she quickly changed her refrain. And she was back to being tough again in an instant. Killian liked that about her.

'So, you had a romantic attachment to Stella Winter?' he pressed.

'That's none of your business,' Cleo snapped, and he could see her eyes welling up again.

'All right, but I had to ask,' Killian said. 'Look, you're not going to like this.'

'Okay, go ahead.' Cleo stood a little more upright.

'How did you know he'd killed her?' Killian looked at her eyes again and they were glossy, but with no tears. 'It only happened a little while ago.'

'Stella and I, we had a connection. As soon as her light burned out, I—I—' She stopped talking and bit back the tears. Then the steeliness returned.

'I felt it.'

'I'm sorry, Cleo, I am, but I can't let you do this with me,' Killian said.

Cleo hardened up in an instant. He could see the fire in her eyes, the passion and the annoyance. 'If you don't let me go in there, then I'll do it on my own,' she insisted and he could tell she was determined.

'Look, you're too invested in this. I don't usually work with anyone and you're... frankly, vulnerable at the moment,' he said.

'What does that mean?' she spat angrily.

'I can't go into a situation with someone who is going to fly off the handle in a second. It's too dangerous for you and me,' Killian said honestly. 'I need someone reliable. Someone who listens to my commands.'

'I can do that. I can,' she insisted. 'Look, Mr Spooks. I don't want to mess this up. I want to do it for Stella. Please, let me help you?' she said and he couldn't resist those beautiful eyes.

He looked at her and sighed. She was changing his mind just by being genuine. He liked that. 'So, you want to help me kill this thing?' Killian said, eyes unblinking.

'Yep. Let's crush this dick and I'll be totally out of your hair, Mr Spooks,' she said. 'That's all I want.'

'Wow. Who's uncouth now? You don't hold back, do you?' Killian could see dogged passion. 'Look, Mr Spooks is my father, not me. Please, call me Killian,' he said with a broad smile. 'Look. I don't know what we're up against in there — I'm sensing something very powerful. To be honest, it scares me.'

'Yeah, me too,' Cleo agreed and chewed her bottom lip. 'This isn't going to be easy.'

'No, it's not,' Killian responded. 'To be fair, I don't know you and you don't know me. We'll have to play it by ear.' Killian knew what power shadow nymphs possessed, but he hadn't seen this girl in action. Now was the time to see for real. 'I don't want you going all gung-ho on me in there. Just follow my lead. Is that clear?' Killian repeated and stared her right in the eyes.

Cleo sighed heavily. 'Yep, got it,' she nodded. 'You're the all-powerful wizard. Let's go and get the wicked witch of the east,' she said with a beaming smile.

Killian shook his head. 'Really, could you be any more condescending?' he said with raised eyebrows.

'Do you want me to answer that, Mr Killian Spooks?' Cleo responded wickedly. 'Sorry, Killian.'

'I guess not. All right, smarty pants, it's time to

get serious and see what you can do,' he said through half-open eyes. He looked at the museum. 'Okay then, let's do this.'

Chapter 6
The Museum

The size of the museum resembled a small castle, which covered a whole block of land. It had two turrets at the front. Nestled on each were ugly, stone gargoyles. They seemed to stare blindly from their blank eye-sockets. Killian gave a shiver. He hated those things. Cleo noticed this and chuckled. He looked at her and shrugged his shoulders as if someone had poured cold water down his back.

'Friends of yours,' she joked, her white teeth gleaming.

Not in a million years, literally,' he said and beamed a smile — she just blinked and rolled her eyes at the irony. Two huge doors secured the building. They were tall and appeared to be made of solid oak. The apex of the arch must have been at least twenty feet high. There was no way Killian could try and force his way through. He lowered his eye-line to halfway down the wooden panels. Right at the centre were two black, twisted iron rings with a keyhole below them. At this point, Killian reached into his pocket and pulled out his pen. Cleo looked at it sceptically but said nothing.

She knew he was a wizard and something really interesting was going to take place. She was right because it morphed into a long, slender silver wand. She hadn't seen it as a pen before it changed. Clever, she thought.

'Very impressive,' she stated.

'Are you going to keep that up all day?' Killian asked with a grunt.

'Yes, if it gets that reaction,' she responded. 'Oh, come on, I'm only kidding.'

'Never work with animals, children or shadow nymphs,' he mumbled.

'I heard that.'

Killian ignored her, and reached out with his left hand and gripped the cold metal ring. It lifted easily and twisted clockwise. He hoped there was a latch on the other side — he was right. They both heard the echoed clunk as the bar lifted from its cradle.

Cleo was standing beside him and he gave her a glance of uncertainty — was it locked though? Killian gave a gentle nudge and to their utter relief, it easily gave way. The wizard closed his eyes and gave a small exhale of breath. He composed himself and before he went any further, he looked again at his new companion.

'Are you ready for this?' he half-whispered and nodded.

'Ready,' she said, now very serious.

He pushed at the giant door and it opened with a long-winded yawn.

'Well, if they didn't know we were coming for them before, then they'll know now,' Cleo said.

'Not my fault,' Killian replied and walked inside. It was initially dark but Killian's wand illuminated the immediate space in front of them. There were a lot of dust particles in the air that resembled a mini snowstorm. Cleo and Killian kept their wits about them by looking in every direction in case the spirit jumper was waiting in the shadows. The foyer was bland, grey and bleak. There was a counter, which was covered in a layer of dust. There was a ledger on top, spread open, and a pen in a holder next to it.

'This place hasn't been used in years,' Killian uttered. On the walls were ancient charts and diagrams of long-lost creatures. To the left of the counter was a turnstile (the type with the rotating bars). The metal bars wouldn't budge when the wizard tried to move one so they quickly and easily climbed over — Killian first and Cleo behind him. They moved through to a much bigger room. This place had many doors and on each one a bronze plaque that depicted what was behind it. First off one read: Stone Age, then Bronze Age and another with the title: War Throughout History. There was also a Rest Room and many other plaques further along. The place was almost completely still, except for the dust particles and cobwebs floating like sails on a boat. Sets along the walls — in the gaps between the various doors — were pedestals with glass cases on top. These had various carcasses of animals inside them.

Killian gave a shiver, even though it was his job to work with strange and weird creatures. This place must have looked scary for little kids with the lights on. In this sweeping darkness, it was positively grim.

'I don't like this place,' Killian admitted in a whisper that swept along the corridor.

'Yeah, let's not stay here a minute longer than we have to. It's creepy in here,' Cleo agreed.

Killian concentrated on the many entrances. Which way should he go? But his mind was made up for him.

A sharp clatter smashed the silence, immediately grabbing their attention. He looked at Cleo and she said nothing but looked back. Killian urgently pointed his wand, but there were too many doors to know exactly where the sound came from. They walked further down the passageway and heard another sound. It seemed to come from behind a door, which had The Animal Kingdom marked on it. Killian nodded.

'I think we've found it,' Cleo said in a whispered tone.

'I think you may be right,' Killian agreed. 'We

go in as quietly as possible. Maybe this thing won't be expecting us and we'll have the element of surprise,' he added and doused the light from his wand. The door held a tarnished, brass hand-plate, which Killian pushed open and they scrambled inside as quietly and quickly as they could. The entrance swept into another long corridor as dark as the foyer. There was no one there so Killian produced his wand again and the tip lit up their immediate area.

'What is it with long corridors in this place,' the wizard complained.

'I know what you mean,' Cleo agreed. They soon came up against yet another door and Killian, as with all the others, doused his wand and carefully opened the door.

They were almost blinded as they entered this part of the building. It was instant, pure daylight and they were completely exposed. It took a few seconds for their eyes to adjust to the brilliance, but they knew they had to hide as quickly as they could. Like a cat, Cleo quietly and swiftly rolled behind a monkey exhibit. The stuffed creatures were set up as a group in a playful jungle setting. They appeared moth-eaten with dull, glassy eyes and grey, dusty fur. Killian slipped behind a large silverback gorilla, which was majestically placed overlooking its domain. That too was rather shabby looking. Killian raised his wand in readiness for a confrontation, the tip crackling with sparks.

Light spilt in from overhead through a dirty, stained glass roof. This room was vast. It appeared as it would have done in its hay day, which by the look of things was in the early seventies. Killian popped his head over the shoulder of the gorilla. It held a musky smell of dust and god knows what else. He tried not to cough and draw attention to himself. He scanned the area and saw Cleo peering back at him.

'Hey, can you see anything?' she called over in a high-pitched whisper.

'Not yet,' Killian admitted. Except for a few flapping birds on the roof, everything was still. When it felt safe, they stepped out from hiding and met on a central pathway. The path was supposed to resemble a curving dirt track, which gave the illusion of walking through a jungle setting. Its intention was to make it feel as real as possible. But the road was just flat, lino flooring with a pattern on it and some loose rock and gravel thrown in. The only real obstacles on it now were mostly bird droppings and the odd branch that had fallen off a plant.

'Do you think it's still in—' But Cleo stopped when they heard a voice deeper inside. Killian put his finger to his lips and gestured for her to follow him. Then he noticed that some of the dirt had been spilt onto the floor. Someone or something had disturbed the carefully laid out displays. He also saw broken branches, which had been ripped from an overhanging tree that divided the path in two directions.

'Come on, this way,' Killian said and pointed to the left.

'Why don't we split up? We can cover more ground that way?' Cleo said sensibly.

'Hold on. I never said anything about splitting up. It's way too dangerous. No, we're much stronger as a team,' Killian specified.

Cleo gave a puff of disapproval. 'Look, if we go one way and then don't find anything,' she said, 'then we'll have to come back to check out the other side. That will waste precious time and it might get away. If we take a side each, then we can call one another for back up.'

Killian looked at her and pondered the thought. It did make a lot of sense but he was putting a lot of trust in his new colleague. He closed his eyes and scratched his forehead. Cleo waited and cleared her throat to get his attention. Killian opened his eyes.

'Okay, but call me if you're in trouble,' Killian said. 'I hope I don't regret this,' he added, in a much quieter voice.

'You won't,' Cleo said and Killian had forgotten that shadow nymphs have superior hearing. 'Look after yourself too,' she responded. They broke off and went their separate ways. Both of them kept low and moved along the floor swiftly. '

'This is nuts,' he grumbled. 'We shouldn't have split up. We need to stay together.' He was already regretting his decision, but it was too late to change anything now. Killian soon slowed when the noise they'd heard earlier was a lot louder. Whatever it was, it wasn't too far away and he could feel his usual tingling. He kept to the artificial foliage for cover and as he got within range, he realised that there was more than one voice talking. It was a conversation. But this was a spirit jumper — a single entity. Who could it be talking to?

'Jesus, why did I agree to splitting up?' he whispered, gnashing his teeth. With two of them, it was going to be more difficult.

The wizard crawled across the ground, his wand still in hand. He came across a large boulder, which obstructed his view. There were also some bushes strategically placed to the side of the rock. He realised that this was set up as a lookout. It was for enthusiasts to see how it would be to spy on the animals in the wild. He peered through the foliage and saw a stuffed hyena, which was hidden in the brush. It had a perfect vantage point to stalk a wildebeest that was drinking at a pond.

But it was another scene which got Killian's attention. He could just make out the figure of the man who had been taken over by the evil spirit jumper. The man was pacing back and forth chanting something. This is strange, he thought. It wasn't a conversation between two people. It was the entity in its turmoil of thought. Killian was fascinated. He hadn't realised that a spirit jumper had a thought process' he'd assumed they just killed and inhabited. He crouched down and kept perfectly still as he tried to listen to what the host was saying. But it was jumbled nonsense. Or "spirit speak", which he'd never had the opportunity to learn. In amongst all the mutterings, and as Killian tried to make sense of it all, his concentration was broken.

Suddenly, police sirens rang through the air and Killian realised that Stella Winter's lifeless body had been discovered in the shopping mall. He leant forward to try and get a better view of his subject, but the fibreglass boulder he pressed against collapsed under his weight and he fell out onto the open floor. He grimaced at his stupidity — there was nowhere to hide.

Chapter 7
Face to Face

Killian quickly looked up and came face to face with the man he'd seen in the image of the essence tracer. But the personality inside the body wasn't there any more. The spirit had engulfed his whole being. Killian felt a twinge of sadness in the pit of his stomach. There was nothing he could do for that poor soul. But there he was — six foot tall and as stiff as an iron rod. His face was pale, drained of any colour as if all the blood had been sucked out. The eyes were the worst — blood-shot, a deep rich scarlet.

The spirit immediately lunged at him. Killian didn't even have time to raise his wand to protect himself. The zombified body knocked him over onto his back and pinned him down by kneeling on his shoulders. It then gripped him around the throat with both its hands. Ordinarily, Killian would have held enough strength to hold himself upright against a mortal man, but this was anything but mortal or even a man. This was a powerful spirit, which drew its strength from the dark side. Killian, on impact, had dropped his wand, and couldn't move to retrieve it. This thing weighed heavy on his body and was squeezing the life out of him.

Killian was choking to death and grabbed its collar, to try and push it off. But he felt light-headed and the oxygen was slowly draining from his lungs.

The spirit jumper was strong and his wild eyes glared as its grip tightened even further around Killian's throat. The demon opened its mouth as wide as it could. Killian could see something manifesting inside its throat—a deep blackened mass—and he realised that the dark matter had already claimed the lives of countless victims. This spurred him into action. He wasn't going to be the next in line.

'Get off me, you fucking freak,' Killian rasped and tried to push it away with all his strength, but it was no use. The charcoal-like fog spilt out of its mouth and poured its way towards the wizard's face. Killian's eyes stretched to their widest as he fought. Soon he could feel the cold vapour drizzle over his face, so he kept his mouth tightly shut. Its wispy tendrils poured over his sealed lips and climbed up towards his nostrils. He knew that if it got fully inside his nose, then that would be the end. Through smart thinking, he let go of the demon's collar and jabbed both thumbs deep into its eye sockets. It felt disgusting and squidgy. He gripped the head and forced his thick thumbs in deeper and deeper.

By now Killian was barely breathing but didn't relent with the pressure to its eye sockets. The monster let go of Killian's throat and he gulped in air hungrily but applied as much pressure as he could. The monster used its hands to grip Killian's wrists and tried to pull them away, but Killian wasn't going to stop now. This was his only chance to survive this. So he dug right in as hard as he could. It was like bursting two hardened grapes and the resistance to his thumbs dissolved in a microsecond. The tips slid inside the sockets and the eyeball's popped. The spirit jumper screamed in excruciating pain — green liquid poured out of each hole in a sticky, disgusting, warm gel. Killian wretched at the stink that followed — it was sickening. The monster pulled away and instantly the dark mist that was making its way inside Killian's airways retracted. Killian pushed the body away and quickly scrambled for his wand. He urgently turned to face the creature again, expecting it to be disorientated. But he stopped and stared and swallowed hard. He couldn't believe what he was witnessing.

The carcass of the man was suspended in mid-air, wrapped up tight in what appeared to be a black smoke-like shawl. He rubbed his eyes to make sure that he wasn't hallucinating — he wasn't. The zombie-like creature was being held by a source, which came from behind. The spirit demon's body wriggled and writhed in an attempt to break free. Killian was confused for a second and craned his neck to look around it. He saw Cleo Smoke standing there. She had both her arms raised and a long, black stream of smoke came directly from her fingertips. She looked in distress and Killian arched his brow.

'I can only hold it for so long, Killian. You'll have to neutralise it now,' she screamed and her voice sounded strained. Killian immediately got to his feet and approached the creature. Its feet were dangling at chest height. The devilish spirit was struggling wildly to break free from Cleo's grip. Killian looked at its eyes – they were just jellified sockets. Killian winced and almost threw up, but managed to keep it down.

'Don't look, Killian. Kill it, just kill the fucking thing,' she screamed. He raised his wand and pointed at the entity. Killian's breathing quickened and he could feel his heart beating against his chest.

'Hold on for as long as you can, Cleo,' he instructed.

'What?' she winced; her voice sounded strangled. 'I can't hold on much longer, Killian.'

'Who brought you here?' Killian demanded. '*Tell me now, demon!*' he bellowed. The entity dropped its head to look the wizard deep in the eyes. It smiled and probed with its empty eye sockets. It was the scariest thing Killian had seen in decades.

'Death is coming, wizard,' the spirit conveyed in a deep and husky pitch.

Killian felt tightness in his stomach. 'Are you kidding me?' Killian said. 'Death is coming. Is that all you can say?'

But the spirit jumper didn't speak any more. It used all its strength to try and break free from Cleo's grasp.

'Killian. I can't hold on much longer. Do something. Do it now, for fuck's sake.' Cleo was strained, a look of anguish across her face.

'You will never return here,' Killian boomed and then pointed his wand at the creature's open mouth. He began conjuring a spell, but as he did so a crack appeared in the ceiling above its body. The fissure manifested into a jagged rip that wasn't of this world. The black swirling mass crackled and sparked. Killian realized immediately what was happening and quickly completed the spell. He unleashed the power of his wand, sending a surge of white energy from the tip. It tore into the corpse, like piranhas attacking prey. The demon shrieked at the pain and part of its body splintered before it was swallowed up completely by the hole. The power generated blew

Killian and Cleo way across the room, shattering windows, doors and levelling everything in sight. Then nothing.

In amongst the rubble came calmness.

Everything appeared quiet for the next few moments. The air was filled with loose debris — dust, papers and fur floated gently to the ground. Killian pushed himself up through a collapsed partition and coughed to clear his throat. He shook his head and dust fell like soot from his brown hair. He got up and scanned the room and couldn't believe the devastation the spirit jumper had caused. There were plants and stuffed animals everywhere. A summer breeze was blowing in through the remains of the glass roof — the place was trashed. As he came around, he remembered his new friend.

'Cleo… Cleo!' Killian shouted. He waited a few moments and was about to call out again when he heard movement. He felt warmth in his heart. At least she was moving, so she must be okay.

'Over here — I'm fine,' Cleo Smoke shouted back. He could see her clamber through the branches of a fallen palm tree. She stepped out into the open and dusted herself down. The two of them made their way back to the foyer and stood in the relative calm of the only area that was virtually untouched. It was a lot lighter in there too as the doors weren't blocking the view any more.

'Did you see where our friend went?' Killian asked urgently and patted down the dust from his jacket. He coughed when the dust hit his throat.

'The last I saw was his body disintegrating before the explosion happened,' she admitted. 'After that everything went black.'

'Yeah, me too, but I saw something weird before I discharged my wand,' Killian explained.

'What did you see?' Cleo quizzed, her eyes widening. Even covered in the dust she was beautiful.

'I think it disappeared,' he said solemnly. 'I'm not a hundred per cent certain, but I think I saw it disappear through the rip.' Killian recalled, 'and after that nothing.'

'It can't go to the other world? No, no, that can't happen,' she said, her blue eyes glistening with fear.

'Yeah. I'm almost positive it got away,' Killian said with remorse. 'I don't think I was quick enough, Cleo, sorry.'

'Well, that's unfortunate,' Cleo said, with her teeth clenched. 'It'll come back for sure.'

'Well, we'll have to deal with that when it happens,' Killian said truthfully. 'Look, whatever has happened, we've got to get out of here. The police are already on their way to investigate the explosion, you can bet. We don't want to be here when they arrive,' Killian said calmly. As he said it so the sound of sirens echoed in the distance.

'Disappearing will be easy for me,' she said with confidence, 'but what about you?'

'Don't worry about me. I've got a friend in the know,' Killian assured her.

'This isn't over,' Cleo said, the bitterness seething through her words. 'I thought I'd done what I came here to do — avenge my friend's death — but that hasn't happened. If you find it, I want to be in on the kill. Promise me you'll keep in contact?'

'Okay,' Killian lied and took a deep breath. Then he watched as she disappeared in a puff of black dust. 'And that's why she's called Cleo Smoke,' he chuckled. He suddenly realised that he didn't have his wand. He patted his pockets and remembered that the last time he'd seen it was just before the explosion. He quickly returned to the main hall and mumbled something and held out his hand. His trusty wand flew through the air and landed in his grip.

Killian looked at it before it turned back into the pen. There was something stuck to the end. He grabbed it and pulled hard to separate it from the wand. It felt as if it was magnetized to it. 'What is this?' Killian mumbled to himself as he examined the object. When he looked closer it appeared to be a black splinter. But what would magnetize itself to his wand? Nothing should stick to it, but then he realised what he was holding and it made him smile.

'This is a fragment of the spirit jumper before it had a chance to escape. It must have broken off and was sucked back towards my wand through its magical charge.' He grinned again. 'Oh, this is precious.' He heard movement outside the building. 'Now, I have to go.' He left through an emergency exit. The police were soon at the scene, but he was long gone.

He ducked out of sight and made his way to the dumpster. There was quite a commotion outside, with police cars and two ambulances. He could hear the siren of a fire engine getting closer too.

He could hear people's excitement. Apparently, not only was there a dead body at the Shambles Shopping Mall, but there was also a gas explosion at the museum too. That would be enough to keep the gossip going for a few days at least. He slipped past everyone unnoticed and ducked out of sight behind the building.

He made his way through the quiet back street with his bike still cloaked. Just walking along, guiding it with his hand and no one suspected. When it was safe enough, he lifted the spell and was soon on the road back home. The air was warm; it felt pleasant after the tussle he'd endured in the museum. As he rode along, he pondered what his next move would be. The spirit jumper had gone, but how did it get here in the first place? And he knew it would be back. He needed to know more about his enemy. And the only thing that could help him was back at his apartment. He needed to consult the "Bowl of Knowledge".

Chapter 8
Cloud Spirit

Killian pulled up outside Glenside and switched off the engine. He wheeled his scooter into the passageway and placed it in a gap under the stairs. He didn't need to use the spell inside—no one would steal it at Glenside. Once he started to relax his body ached. He found new places that hurt when he stood and stretched his back. He took in a deep breath and exhaled with a long sigh. He could hear the machines pumping away in the background; this always brought a smile to his face for some reason.

He wearily clambered up the flight of stairs and made his way past the office into his apartment. Before he'd even had time to get a cup of coffee the phone rang, and he ground his teeth with displeasure. It was late afternoon by now and he was tired. He had things to do, but a shower was first on the agenda.

'I'm going to have to get Glyn to put an extension in this room at some point,' he groaned. He picked up the receiver and the smooth, silky tone of Penny White's voice washed over him. He forgot about his fatigue in an instant.

'Mr Spooks, it's Penny White,' she said very formally. 'I've been trying to call you all afternoon.' She sounded annoyed. 'Don't you have a mobile phone?'

'Please, call me Killian,' he reminded her. 'No, I don't have a mobile,' he lied, not wanting to have the conversation about his special mobile.

'Ah, okay… Killian.' she still found it difficult saying his name. 'I thought everyone carried a phone these days, oh well,' she said and paused for a moment before continuing. 'I need an update on the case for my boss.'

'Oh, all right. Mmmm,' he mumbled. 'Things have taken a turn in another direction,' he said honestly.

'What do you mean,' she asked, sounding sceptical, 'another direction?'

'Look. I can't discuss this over the phone,' Killian replied. 'It's a bit complicated, um, you understand?'

'Yes, okay. What if we meet up?' Penny said and felt a little awkward as she said it. 'I mean, er, to discuss the case, over a drink,' she uttered, trying not to sound embarrassed. 'I mean to discuss things — tea, coffee, alcohol. Oh God, this is coming out all wrong.'

She was flustered and Killian loved that about her. 'Are you sure you're not asking me out on a date, Miss White?' Killian teased, rubbing it in a little.

'No! Definitely not, Mr Spooks... I mean, Killian... I mean, er, not a date.' She was tripping over every word and Killian let her squirm. He grinned on the other end of the phone, but tried not to chuckle. He could picture her cute little cheeks turning a rosy red and her nose wrinkling up. He couldn't help but finally let out a chuckle — deep in his throat.

'Are you making fun of me, Mr Spooks?' she sounded annoyed. 'You are making fun of me.'

'Oh, calm down, Miss White,' Killian said. 'Can't you take a joke? I'm only winding you up,' he said in a softer tone.

'Why, yes, of course you are,' she replied. 'I'm sorry if I took it the wrong way. I'm not very good at this, am I?' She didn't normally banter with people. This was all new to her and she kind of liked it.

'No problem. Say around seven then at the Square Inn, Miss White, does that suit you?' Killian asked.

There was silence for a second or two and then she spoke. 'Penny,' she replied in a much more calm and soothing tone.

'I'm sorry,' Killian was puzzled.

'Please, call me Penny?' she asked in a cheerier tone. 'Miss White is so formal and we are working together now.'

'Oh, I see. All right. I'll see you at seven, Penny?' Killian responded and felt the happiest he'd felt in a while.

'I'll see you there... Killian.' She said his name and dropped an octave, before putting down the receiver. He moved the phone from his ear and gave it a long, lingering stare of disbelief. Why were women so complicated, he pondered, before putting the phone in its cradle. He soon snapped back to reality and regained focus. He realised what he had to do.

'Okay,' he said to himself and scratched the bristles on his chin. Killian went back into his living room and made his way to the back. There, he put his two hands on the bookcase... and pushed. The wooden panel gave way and swung open silently. The wizard stepped through to the next room and pulled on a cord, which lit a single light bulb. The brightness hurt his eyes for a moment and he squinted. Once he could focus again, he looked around. This room was empty and had no windows. It had once housed Glyn's cash safe. And he thought it prudent to have a room hidden away, just in case someone broke into his property. No one would even think of a place back there. The safe itself had been long removed and all that remained now were a stack of shelves. They were full with jars, bottles and vials lined up in perfect order, with all the labels facing outwards. Inside each vessel were liquids of many colours and various other plant roots, leaves and powders.

In the centre of the room was a large object covered in a dustsheet. Killian grinned with half open eyes. He pulled back on the material and released a cloud of dust into the air, making it just that little bit harder to breathe. He coughed as he rolled up the sheet and discarded it to one side of the room. Left in its place was an ordinary, wooden cupboard, with two drawers on top and two doors underneath. Killian had brought this piece of furniture with him when he'd first moved in.

Placed in the centre at the top of the cupboard was a silver dish, with a space each side. The dish was the size and shape of a dessert tureen you'd find in any wedding reception. It was mostly plain, polished silver, but had engraving around the brim on the outside. The pattern was an ancient script, which only a few could read. This was a sacred vessel. Killian stood and marvelled at it. It never failed to excite him every time he revealed it. He didn't use it that often, but this was a time when he needed it most. He walked back out of the room and returned a short time later, with a kettle full of water. He poured the contents into the bowl and placed the kettle back in his small kitchen. He then went to his library and selected a book. It was leatherbound with no title on the cover. This was Killian's notebook and contained all the spells and potions he'd picked up over the years.

He needed a whole bunch of ingredients to mix. He needed to measure everything to perfection before he could discover the whereabouts of the evil power that was disrupting his world. His eyes sparkled when he found what he was looking for. He smiled and took a deep breath and got to work.

Killian placed the open book on the counter next to the bowl. The ingredients he needed were all there in the labelled jars facing him. He ran his finger down the list and looked up at the jars and bottles. The yellow glow from the light bulb gave his face a ghostly appearance. He closed his eyes and muttered with a few mmms and aahs and nodded now and again. He needed to picture the whole process in his head before he did the full sequence. He meditated for a short while as he always did — rolling his head from side to side — and then he stopped. His eyes blinked open and his brow furrowed.

'Okay. I think I've got it,' he said quietly. He looked around the room. 'I need to get more light in here at some point,' he reasoned. He was ready to start.

He selected various vessels and jars and one-by-one either poured liquid straight into the bowl or used different sized spoons, which he took from one of the drawers. He used these to measure and sprinkle in the mixture. The strange thing was that the water didn't change from its natural, clear colour. It stayed perfectly transparent. When Killian had finished, he looked on admiringly at what he'd achieved. Which, if anyone else had seen the bowl, they would probably have thought that it was just filled with ordinary tap water.

Killian stood looking at the tureen, his face half covered in shadow. He knew he had to choose his words very carefully. He only had one shot at this, to get it right. If he asked the wrong question then the bowl of knowledge wouldn't continue with the line of communication and Killian would have to start all over again. That had happened once before and it was imperative back then to get it right, so from then on, he made sure. He took a deep breath and cleared his throat and spoke.

'I am Killian Spooks, wizard of Sloon. I have the right as sorcerer to open a channel between this world and the next.' Killian said and waited for... something, or anything, to happen.

The water didn't move and the wizard felt a sinking feeling in the pit of his stomach. What had he done wrong? He was about to open his mouth to ask again, when the water began to ripple. Killian's face lit up and the excitement brought with it a wide grin.

He studied the bowl and the surface of the liquid changed from a gentle movement to a full-blown bubbling pot. From the disturbance came a vapour, which eventually thickened into mist. At that point Killian stepped back. The mist evolved into a fog, which became a frothy cloud of sorts. The cloud lifted about a metre above the rim and settled for a moment. In its suspended state, images began to appear. Killian was pleased because he knew that he'd achieved the perfect potion. The white, fluffy cloud evolved into a ghostly face. The mouth opened to speak, cutting a large gash in the smoky apparition. Its eyes were just darkened holes that showed the other side of the room, but it made for an eerie sight. And then it spoke.

'Killian Spooks, wizard of Sloon, what is it you seek?' the cloud spirit asked. Killian slipped his hand into his pocket and produced the slither of black rock. He dropped it into the bowl and it fizzed as it hit the surface of the water.

'What do you know of this creature?' Killian asked and waited. The face deliberated for a moment, taking in the substance that the wizard had dropped in.

'This is the one you seek.' The voice from the bowl spoke.

Killian looked on in total concentration.

'Yes. This is the one,' Killian said with a nod and waited, his body tensed.

'This is *Relic*,' the voice explained.

Killian squinted as if he'd heard of this creature before somewhere, but couldn't quite place it. The face in the mist soon changed into another image that moved as a human being, but it did not stay stable and swirled into different shapes and then back to the face in the mist.

'Relic!' Killian said the name and dug deep into his past, but it didn't ring a bell. 'Who is he?' he asked and realised straight away — it was a stupid question. It could never be a mortal person.

'Relic is not a person. Relic is a supernatural force. A dark and dangerous force.'

'How can I stop it?' Killian pressed, hoping that the bowl had some kind of answer. 'Can Relic be stopped?' he added.

'The answer to that question is yes, but it will be difficult. Relic appears and disappears at various times. You have an opportunity on its next appearance, but, if you fail, you may never have another,' the bowl warned. 'Relic causes devastation in one world, then moves on to the next.'

'When is its next appearance?' Killian hoped it would be soon, so he could sort this out once and for all. He knew the fragment he'd put into the water would give the host away.

'Relic will appear tomorrow night. It will show itself at the midnight hour,' the bowl informed him.

'Where will it appear?' Killian asked eagerly.

'Relic will emerge under the arch at Devil's Bridge. Once it has materialised, it will then make an opening between the two worlds, for any force to invade this world.'

Killian was filled with torment. If that happened, then all manner of evil could cross over. 'Thank you, cloud spirit,' he said humbly and soon after that the mist disappeared and the water became calm again. The room was once again settled in silence.

'Wow,' Killian gulped, 'so I've got to seal up the opening, so that nothing else comes through. And... somehow banish Relic from this world never to return — piece of cake,' he joked. 'I'll need help for this,' he said.

Killian looked into the bowl and realised that he needed to know exactly where the entity was going to manifest itself at the bridge. He picked up the stainless-steel basin and took it to the sink. He grabbed a coffee filter pad and a sieve. Next, he found another bowl and placed the sieve over that and put the filter inside the sieve. He emptied the water into the coffee filter and let it filter through to the other bowl. Eventually what was left was dry black sediment. Once the water was removed that substance changed into tiny particles, which the wizard gently emptied into a vial he had from his room. He screwed on the top and looked through the glass for a few moments and took a deep breath, biting his bottom lip in thought. He poured the excess water from the bowl into the kitchen sink. Killian then grabbed a box of matches and set fire to the coffee filter, which quickly ignited in a flash and was gone. The vial, Killian put carefully to one side for now.

Killian sat back on his sofa and pondered. He already knew whom he had to call for advice, but didn't know if he could help or not. He had to try, though, and grabbed his phone. After that, Killian gently put the book back in the bookcase. And finally, he replaced the dustsheet over the bowl and cupboard. He switched off the light and whilst he was closing the door panel to his secret room, he remembered something. 'I have a date with the delicious Miss Penny White.' This lightened the mood somewhat.

Chapter 9
Windy Vale Park

It had been one of the warmest summers in quite a while and that's why Killian decided to take the long route to the pub. One thing he loved about Windy Vale was the fact that it had a particularly nice park.

It was one of those places where you could stroll through and just think. The words from the cloud spirit were still whirling around in his head. This was one of the toughest cases he'd come across, and that was saying something. He decided to try and switch off thinking about his work and just enjoy the tranquil atmosphere of the park.

He loved this place. The grounds were always well kept and manicured to perfection. He always nodded to the groundsman, Harry—a gentleman in his early sixties and with a manner smooth as butter. He couldn't see him anywhere today. He walked by the bowling green and saw a small group of people using it. They were very smartly dressed in their whites. There was a mixture on each team—children, middle-aged and pensioners. The game had never appealed to

Killian, but they seemed to be enjoying it.

The tennis courts were empty, but there again Wimbledon had ended a month or so earlier. He'd noticed that there was always a pattern of the courts being fully booked during the tournament, and then kids just got bored and went back to their video games. He smiled at that thought.

He ambled passed the duck pond. The air soon lifted with excited screams and laughter from children and parents in the play area. There were ball games on the green with a frisbee being tossed. They still did the frisbee thing, Killian smiled.

He continued on further and left the screams and shouts behind. The air was soon filled with the heady perfume of flowers, followed by the pungent aroma of salty, sea air. Killian understood that Windy Vale was a small coastal town and had its own bay. But he'd never gone there. He hated that smell; it gave him a headache. Killian walked through to the quieter, wooded area. A path cut through the trees, making this part of the park more secluded and a little darker, filtering out the strong sunlight through the branches. He came to a fork in the trees where the path went left and right. He'd always taken the right one, which eventually led to the main road and on to the Square Inn. He'd always told himself that one day he would explore the left, just for devilment. This was one of those days and he felt ambitious. He was about to take a step when he was smashed from behind. The impact knocked him off balance and sent him tumbling to the ground.

It all happened so fast and he was disorientated for a few seconds. He turned to see a figure on a bike speeding away. It was making for the left path and he realised what had just happened. Killian immediately dipped his hand into his jacket pocket and found that his wallet was missing. How stupid. He'd read that there were pickpockets working in the area, but didn't think he'd be a victim.

'You little fucker, come back here,' Killian rasped, his back aching. But the intruder was gone in a flash.! Killian got up, feeling slightly unsteady, but he knew that he didn't have much time and broke into a sprint. He was feeling light-headed, but that was the least of his problems right then. He dug in his pocket and pulled out his pen, which immediately morphed into his wand. He ran along the pathway—it twisted from left to right—his lungs already gasping for air and the blood pumping in his head. He could just about hear the wheels whirring and the chain clanking in the stillness of the trees.

He knew he had to act fast and he needed a clear shot. Killian ran at full-pelt until the pathway opened up into a clearing, which made it all the easier to spot the thief. He stopped and bent over gasping for breath with the sweat was soaking his shirt and trickling down his face. It was a hot evening and his head felt as though someone was attacking him with a sledgehammer. He swallowed hard and took another gulp of air. He spotted the biker, peddling for all he or she was worth, hood over their head and zooming along, thinking that they weren't going to get caught. Killian ran the numbers in his head. Nine times out of ten, thieves get away before the victims even knew they'd been robbed. But Killian was damned sure he wasn't going to let this go.

Luckily for him, there was a steady, drop in the pathway in front of him. And he could see, through a haze of gnats, that the path rolled downhill and then swooped into an incline on the other side. He knew that there was no way that he could catch up just by running after the culprit. But he did know that the biker would have to peddle for all they were worth to get to the top, on the other side. And he also understood that once they'd made it there, then that would be it. They could disappear into the treeline and that would be the last he'd see of his wallet.

But he also knew that once the thief was more or less level with Killian's position on the other side, the scumbag would be at his or her slowest — that would be Killian's chance. He spat the insects from his mouth and itched his head and waited. He could barely focus as his head pounded.

'Stop there, you little prick,' Killian shouted angrily, still panting. 'That's my wallet you've stolen. Give it back now while you still have the chance,' he commanded. The person on the bike was still pumping away on the pedals and must have thought, what an idiot. Killian had a good view and could plainly see the kid on the bike. The culprit was the typical stereotype. The obligatory black hoodie, baggy jeans and trainers, all the costume for a thug. But Killian was mad with himself for being hoodwinked in the first place. 'You're losing your edge,' he said in his head. The wizard prepared himself, with arm raised and wand extended. The stinging sweat was pouring into his eyes and his head was thump, thump, thumping, but he stood poised.

Then the idiot made the biggest mistake of their career. Killian was not expecting what happened next. Instead of just riding away and concentrating on their escape — the person got a bit cocky. The biker slowed at the top of the hill and still holding on to the handlebar, to guide the bike, the knob-head stretched out their left arm and gave Killian the bird with their middle finger. No doubt with a cheeky grin under that hood.

Killian gave out a hearty giggle. 'Cheeky, little shit,' he said softly, 'and what a fool.' That's all he needed. Killian quietly mumbled a spell as he pointed his wand directly at the figure. He fired invisible energy from his wand, which instantly hit both rider and the bike.

Killian stood staring, his face a picture of delight. The moment of impact and the thief froze to the spot. It looked really amusing. The guy in the hoodie, still with an arm sticking out doing the rude gesture, but totally locked in a statue-like pose. It was priceless.

Killian urgently looked all around to make sure no one was watching. He didn't need witnesses and anyone could pop along at any moment. He was safe for now though — there was only the two of them in this part of the park. His headache eased slightly and he quickly walked down the steep slope and up the other side. He finally closed in. He grabbed the hood and pulled it back. Killian had the shock of his life. It was a young girl of about twelve or thirteen. He gave a sigh and shook his head. She had mousy hair and dark eyeliner like a Goth. She was quite pretty under all that make-up. They were the ones that looked cute but were sneaky.

Killian knew that the spell had almost completely paralysed its victim. But he also knew that she would still be conscious of what was going on around her. And that would be scary enough. One minute she was doing her thing and stealing someone's belongings and making herself richer in the process. The next minute she was frozen like a statue and wondering what the world was doing to her. It was a cruel but necessary spell. He couldn't help but feel sorry for her, but what about all those people she'd robbed. Taken their hard-earned cash just by stealing it, too easy. No, he didn't regret what he'd done.

'So, little miss, you thought you'd steal my wallet and get away with it, did you?' he said calmly, but with his head still thumping. He could hear her trying to speak as if gagged. She looked terrified. 'Nope. This is not a practice you should be doing,' Killian said and searched the pockets of her hoodie. He fished out his wallet. She totally didn't have time to take anything. And probably didn't even expect him to chase after her either. The wizard coolly put his wallet back in his pocket and leaned in, right to her face. He looked her in the eye and spoke with a low growl. 'If I e-v-e-r,' and he emphasized the word, 'see you doing this again, or find out that you have, I'll know who to look for. But I won't just report you to the police,' he said and with that added a touch of magic, turning his face from his normal appearance into her deepest and darkest nightmare, then back in a split second.

Her eyes bulged and sweat trickled down her brow. She was terrified.

'Now, get the rest of the stuff you've stolen and hand them into the "lost and found". And get lost, kid, before I really lose my temper,' Killian growled, and with that, she and the bike were released from the spell. She immediately toppled over onto the grass in a tangle of bike wheels, legs and arms. Still shaking, she got to her feet and picked up the bike. She was breathing heavily and her eyes looked as though they were about to pop out of her head. Killian could see her whole body, trembling and he could hear her sobbing from deep within her throat. 'Tell the police what happened here if you want, but who's going to believe you, kid?' Killian said, with a grin. 'They've probably got you on file anyway,' he added. 'Now go!'

The girl quickly mounted her bike and sped off as fast as her legs could pump the pedals. In a couple of seconds, she was gone, like a distant memory. Killian made his way back to the fork in the path but felt some sadness in what he'd done. He then hardened up when he realised that if she'd got away with it, she'd have done it again and again.

He decided to go back home take some tablets for his sore head and have a quick shower and change again. His shirt was soaking and he was going on a date and couldn't smell of perspiration. He knew that Penny would be immaculate.

Luckily, he'd given himself plenty of time to have a pint, before he met Penny for a drink. So, now he'd have to sort himself out and make it to the pub at the same time as his meeting. He didn't take long to get back home and ready himself. Soon he was walking by the park again. This time though he decided to skip that little trip, remembering what had happened earlier and made straight for the Square Inn. What would this night bring, he pondered?

Chapter 10
Square Inn

Killian got to the bar just before seven and she hadn't arrived yet. He bought himself a pint of Cambrian and sat in deep thought, his head filled with the entity called Relic. He had to fill Chief Hathaway in on what had already taken place by telling Penny when she turned up. After that, he had to get in touch with his friend, Zoot. Killian hated it when he didn't know what his opponent was capable of, but he did know that this one was a really powerful and unpredictable force. Zoot was the only one who could help. And Zoot may have even come into contact with this creature in the past.

'Killian, Killian.' He heard his name being called, but it didn't register for a couple of seconds. Until he realised that Penny White was standing right there in front of him.

'Oh, sorry, Miss White—' but she widened her eyes waiting for a response. 'Sorry,' he repeated, recognising his mistake, 'Penny.' He remembered that she preferred to be called by her first name. Killian rarely got too personal with his clients and this all felt a bit strange, but nice. 'What would you like to drink, Penny?' he asked as he looked up at her.

'I'll have a glass of prosecco, please,' she said, with a cheeky grin. Killian was going to feel awkward about ordering at the bar. He only ever bought his beer and didn't order drinks for other people.

'No problem,' he lied. 'I'll be back in a tick. Please, take a seat,' he gestured to the padded, leather bench at the opposite side of the table. He felt vulnerable, but he was a wizard, for God's sake. A wizard, who faced the supernatural every day, but was awkward around women in general. He could banter with them, yes, but when it came to a real one-to-one conversation, he'd rather face a deadly enemy with six heads that secreted venom than talk to someone on the other side of the table. He ordered her drink and looked around the bar. The Square Inn was quite a popular place. The pub staff flitted like busy bees, serving meals at the multitude of tables. To add to their misery was a spiral staircase that led to a second floor. It was always pretty loud, too; that was why Killian liked it, because of the anonymity. No one bothered him. There were all types of people that came here: professionals having meetings or just meeting up after work, and the regulars who propped up the counter and never seemed to leave.

Killian's eyes came to a rest on Penny as she dug around in her bag. She was even prettier in civilian clothes, if that were possible. Her thick, black hair perfectly framed her face and draped her shoulders. She wore a purple, flower print dress with thin straps that showed a fair portion of her shoulders. Killian discreetly looked at her deep, sumptuous cleavage before eventually moving to her waist, which was petite. He noticed when he looked further that the hem fell just above her knee, revealing slim, tanned legs. It took all he had to stop himself from actually drooling. She was gorgeous.

'Your drink, mate.' Killian broke focus and turned to the bartender.

'Yeah, thanks,' he said and picked up the glass and grabbed his change. He then dodged his way back to Penny and placed the glass in front of her. She glanced up at him and smiled. Then he noticed the notepad and pen next to the beer mat. So this is an official meeting, not a date, he thought. He felt betrayed somehow; it had sounded different over the phone, more friendly than business. Ah well, he pondered, let's get this over with.

'You want a report,' he said arching his brow. She looked at him with slight confusion and then followed the line of his sight to the pad.

'Uh,' she stumbled, 'well, this is a meeting,

right?'

'Of course it is,' Killian said in a condescending tone. His thoughts of a nice evening of friendly conversation, and maybe a goodnight kiss, soon disappeared. He put his official head on and sank into the mind-set of the case. 'Okay.'

'Sorry to interrupt.' Penny picked up on his tone and cut in with a raised finger to clarify, so Killian stopped and looked into her beautiful, azure eyes.

'Yeah,' he responded.

'You thought this was more than a meeting?' she said and creased her brow.

'No. Not at all,' he lied. 'Did you?'

'Uh, oh, n-no, of course not,' she said, dismissing the idea altogether.

'Let's get on with this *meeting* then,' he said, emphasizing the word so it stood out. The atmosphere went from friendly to an official meeting in one gigantic swoop; both now felt very uncomfortable. Penny, instead of leaning in with her elbows on the table, now sat more upright and grabbed her pen and pad. This date was going downhill in free-fall. Killian took a deep breath and looked at her while trying to move his mouth, but not saying anything.

'What?' she asked. Her nose wrinkled — he loved that.

'I'm just trying to figure out where to start,' he said truthfully, trying to take his mind away from what he wanted to do. He started. 'That gas explosion at the museum,' he said. Penny looked at him and nodded, immediately recollecting the earlier incident. 'And Stella Winters's body at the Shambles and—'

'The charcoaled bodies at Stella Winters's house,' Penny interrupted, looking directly into his eyes.

'Yep, they are all connected,' Killian admitted with a nod.

'The museum wasn't a gas leak then?' Penny asked, intrigued. 'Wow!'

'Nope. That was the spirit jumper,' Killian said, his eyes wide and fully into the discussion.

'Spirit jumper?' Penny looked confused. Killian sighed. 'What's a spirit jumper?'

'I haven't explained very well, have I?' he said. Penny just shook her head. 'The thing—the being, the entity—call it what you will. It's a spirit from the other side that's causing all the attacks and deaths in Windy Vale,' Killian revealed. 'It can take over people's personalities and consume their bodies and use them for what it wants. Then, once it doesn't want that person any more—it moves on to the next,' he explained.

'Wow, that's horrible. Hold on a minute. Let me get this straight in my head because I have to report all this stuff to my boss,' Penny said, shaking her head with confusion. 'The guy who got killed, not too far from here, Toady Williams?' she said and looked serious and professional.

'Shhh, keep your voice down in here,' Killian warned and put his finger to his lips.

'Oops sorry,' she apologised and lowered her voice. 'Toady Williams and the hen party he attacked, including Stella Winter, who I presume has attacked some other poor soul and now she's dead, too,' Penny added, 'this is the work of a spirit that takes over bodies and then discards them and moves on to the next? This is a lot to take in,' Penny looked confused.

'In a nutshell, and you're right. It is a lot to swallow,' Killian agreed.

Penny put down her pad and pen and rested her forehead in her right hand. She picked up her wine glass, took a sip and put it down. Killian could see her pink lipstick on the rim of the glass.

'How on earth am I going to explain this to Chief Inspector Hathaway?' She appeared distraught.

'You don't believe me... do you?' Killian retorted in a sigh. If he was honest with himself, it did all sound unbelievable, especially to the likes of the mortal world — like a plot for a bad horror movie. 'I...' Killian sighed again. 'I can see it's difficult to take in,' he said, and his face told a story of someone who had tried to explain this many times before. 'But it's all true, really, honestly,' he said.

Penny looked deep into his eyes and she could see, heart-of-hearts, that he was telling the truth as far as he believed. And, she had to weigh-up the situations of the deaths that couldn't be explained by the police department. The fact was that her boss, Hathaway, was at a loss as to how to continue with any of this investigation. This was the reason he'd chosen Killian Spooks in the first place. And if she was honest with herself, she liked this guy. He was dishevelled and disorganised, all the opposites that she normally wouldn't go anywhere near. But he was gorgeous and, she could see, extremely serious about his work too.

'Okay,' she said, 'what next?' He looked at her and a broad smile lifted his tired face.

'So you do believe me?' he concluded, and he too gulped his pint.

'It's going to be a damn weird conversation with Hathaway, but yes, I do,' she admitted.

'The gas explosion wasn't anything to do with gas — as you've probably guessed by now. It was just explained away like that so that no one had to do any out of the ordinary reports, probably,' he said. 'But what really happened, Penny.' She leaned in. 'This spirit jumper opened up a void from this world to the next.'

'Next?' Penny gasped.

'Yeah, the land of the dead.' He looked at her to see if she was still following. 'I may mess with you at times, but I'm not joking on this one.'

'Wow,' she was shocked, but looked interested this time.

'It has a name,' Killian revealed. 'It's called Relic and it regrettably escaped from the museum.' Penny didn't speak, only concentrated. 'There's a charcoaled body in there somewhere of a young man. I was there trying to capture and banish Relic back to the dark world. He nearly got me, too.'

'So, what happens now?' Penny probed.

'I know where and when Relic will appear next,' Killian said confidently.

'That's great,' Penny interrupted. 'I can let Hathaway know and he can have an armed response unit on the scene waiting for him,' she said.

'Oh… no, no, Penny. I have to deal with this. We're talking about forces here that no mortal can comprehend. Bullets and tasers won't have any effect against this force,' Killian said seriously.

'No mortal…' Penny's belief was starting to waver.

'Look, you either believe me, or you don't?' Killian said angrily. She could see she'd hurt him.

'I'm sorry Killian — please continue,' she apologised. Killian took a moment to compose himself.

'I need to confront it and send it back so that it can't reappear again. And I can't do that with the police all over the place. It'll go sideways in no time and their weapons will be futile, believe me' he said, raising his voice, his chest heaving with the anger he felt.

'Okay, okay. I'll leave it to you. I'm sorry,' she said, her face stern. 'But I've got to send a report to Hathaway on this. It's going to be difficult to explain; he knows weird things are going on, but he needs answers. He's got the mayor badgering him for information because there's an election coming up.' She rolled her eyes. 'Hathaway is already breathing down my neck.' She gripped her glass, her fingers white at the knuckles. The tension between her and Killian became toxic; the chemistry gone.

Killian stood up, breathing hard. 'Look. Make your report and I'll hopefully get this sorted in the next couple of days,' he responded, with no emotion. 'I have to go, Penny,' he said regrettably, and looked at her, his eyes filled with torment.

She gazed back, not expecting his sudden departure.

'Oh, okay,' she said. Her face showed the disappointment that weighed on her stomach. 'Keep me up to speed, will you?' Her voice tapered off.

'I will,' Killian said and finished off his drink. He walked away and left her sitting there. Penny could feel the tears build in her eyes as she watched him walk out the door. She gulped her drink and swallowed it down in one go. She wiped her mouth with the back of her hand, smudging her lipstick. Then she got up and left, holding back the tears.

Killian got back to his flat and slumped onto his sofa. He couldn't get the image of Penny's distraught face out of his mind. He'd left her on her own and upset. Why did he do that? Admittedly he was tired and recent events had taken their toll, but that was no reason or excuse to end their meeting the way he did. He eased back on the sofa and closed his eyes. He soon drifted into a deep slumber.

Chapter 11
Zoot

The next day Killian woke to find himself still on the settee. The first thoughts that came to his mind were that of Penny's distraught face at the table and he felt bad. He shook away her face from his thoughts and took a shower. He made a coffee and something to eat before heading off. It was another beautiful summer morning in Windy Vale. He fired up the Vespa and drove to the edge of town. It was ten-thirty and the sun was already high. The heat of the day was building and, combined with the hot engine, made it almost unbearable to drive in trousers and a jacket. He pulled into a petrol station and began filling up the small tank. Another reason he loved his scooter was that they could almost go forever on a tankful of gas. He'd had a couple of dry spells lately with no cases and the money was low, so having something so economical was essential. He looked to the mountain while he was pumping in the fuel. Zoot lived high on a hill, far away from the population.

After paying, Killian jumped on his scooter and took a deep breath before he put on his helmet.

Above the fumes of petrol, he caught a fresh, hint of spruce and pine from the forest. He started his bike and drove off. Once he left the main road, he could feel the Vespa strain as it climbed up the long gradient to the clouds, or so it felt. The musky odour of fern and the heady, sharp smell of the pine dominated the air. Zoot's house was quite a big affair, set in the middle of a field. There was a rough, stone-laden road that led to his front gate. The bumpy ground was a deterrent mostly. Zoot didn't like uninvited visitors — he was a social recluse. So Killian had to ring ahead to let him know he was coming before he could have permission to visit.

Killian sped across the loose shale and clouds of white dust billowed in his wake. He lifted his visor and the cool air that buffeted his face was welcome after the heat inside the helmet. He slowed as he got to the wooden gate and switched off the scooter. He then pulled it back on its stand and stood for a moment, to look at the house. He hadn't been here in quite a while — Zoot wasn't someone you visited often. He shook his head in disbelief — it was a truly amazing sight. Everything in and around the house was pristine, from the well-manicured garden to the brilliant white of the wooden walls. The house had eight bedrooms and many windows. There were wooden arched doorways, on either side of the building. These led to the rear lawns and the beautiful river that flowed through the grounds. Everywhere were the chimes and symbols of ancient gods and strange animals. Zoot was a great believer in the power of the ancients and the mysteries of the animal form. You instantly felt at ease here, as if nothing else mattered. This place was a definite polar opposite to the hustle and bustle of the town. It was so peaceful, too, apart from the tinkling of hanging ornaments.

Zoot was an unusual character with a very special power of his own. Killian needed that special power to help him with the particular problem that he faced. He could have stood there all day, but time was against him and he needed to speak to Zoot right away. So he placed his helmet on the seat and walked past the gate and up the path. He stepped on the porch and ducked this way and that, to avoid the dangling wind chimes. If he lived here this would drive him mad. He grinned and shook his head.

Killian was about to knock on the door when it slid open automatically. That's new he thought, he didn't remember that when he came last time.

'Zoot... Zoot,' he called out, but there was no reply. The wizard walked over the threshold and inside. It had been a while since he'd entered Zoot's house and it hadn't changed a bit. It was all white walls and soft furnishings, all very zen. The sofa in the living room was a big L-shaped affair in white leather with orange cushions, and set inside the L was a long, marble coffee table, also in white with a thin, grey-veined, pattern running through it. On the walls were framed, mythical animals: dragons, griffins, serpents and others that he couldn't name. He stood and gazed admiringly at the pictures.

'It's been a while, Killian. Please, take a seat.' Killian instantly relaxed at the soft, velvet tones of Zoot's voice. He stood at the doorway carrying a large, white tray with a teapot and china cups on top. This also made Killian smile. The only time he drank tea was when he came up here to visit his old friend.

Zoot was of medium height with a polished, bald head and a long, orange robe, which always reminded Killian of a Tibetan monk. It wouldn't seem out of place in a monastery, but here in Windy Vale, it was definitely different. Killian, though, liked old Bruce Lee movies and expected ninjas to attack at any minute. He gave a broad smile. Zoot smiled back. His face was as smooth as the marbled table, but his eyes were hypnotic. They were brown in colour and translucent; you never knew what he was thinking. He was quite a handsome chap and wearing his orange garment gave him a different look from everyone else. He'd look more in place handing out leaflets on the street with the theme of peace and love. Not that Zoot would go anywhere near the streets of Windy Vale.

'Thank you, Zoot. Thank you for seeing me,' Killian said politely. 'I know you don't take visitors lightly.' Zoot rested the tray on the table and began the task of setting up the cups and pouring the milk and tea, adding sugar. When he'd finished, he handed a beautiful bone china cup and saucer to the wizard.

'You sounded agitated on the phone. What can I do for you, Killian?' Zoot asked, his voice calm. 'It must be serious, I knew as soon as I heard your voice.'

'Well, I do have a rather severe problem and I was wondering if you could give me advice or even help me to deal with it,' Killian asked. 'I wouldn't have called otherwise. I know you like to be left alone to your thoughts.'

'That's not entirely true, Killian. I love it when you visit. You are one of my oldest and most cherished friends,' Zoot said with sincerity and his eyes sparkled. 'What's the problem?'

'I was asked to investigate a case by the police chief. I found a disturbance in the supernatural world. There is a being that wants to penetrate this world and bring evil with it,' Killian explained, as he put the cup and saucer down on the table.

'And what do you want to ask me?' Zoot

113

peered deep into Killian's eyes. It was almost a hypnotic experience. Killian shook his head to break out of it.

'Can you help me stop it. Or will you show me a way of stopping it?' the sorcerer asked bluntly. 'It's more than I can handle.'

'You don't hold back, do you?' Zoot replied.

'Nope. No point,' Killian said.

'In fact, that's what I like about you, wizard. You tell it like it is and are truthful. I can help you, but stopping it… I don't know.' Zoot appeared agitated now and that shook Killian to the core. Was he scared? Killian had never known Zoot to be scared of anything.

'What is it, Zoot?' Killian questioned. 'Are you okay? Tell me. You know something, I can tell.' Killian was so fired up that he was leaning over in his seat.

'What is coming is far more powerful than I,' Zoot admitted. 'I have felt it,' he explained. 'I haven't felt anything like this for a long time. I was expecting your call. I have to get involved in this because it threatens everything in our world. We can face this together, Killian.'

Killian was relieved. Zoot's help could prove to be the one thing he needed to overcome the situation. Relic couldn't be allowed to roam this world freely and bring God knows what with it. Killian relaxed and sat back on the sofa.

'Thank you,' Killian said as he sipped his tea. He didn't have to face this alone now. 'This supernatural being is called —' Killian was about to say, but Zoot stopped him there with a wave of his hand.

'I don't want to know anything until we're there, Killian. I can pick up on what's happening and maybe work something out on the spot,' Zoot said smartly. 'If I know beforehand then...' Zoot was about to continue when he felt better of it. 'Let's just work it out when we get there.'

'Are you sure? Don't you want to know what you're dealing with? I certainly would,' Killian admitted.

Zoot stood there shaking his head. 'No,' came his dismissive reply. Killian realised they'd been friends for a long time and trusted his judgment. 'Whatever this thing is, I'm better off learning about it there and then.'

'Okay,' Killian said, 'if that's the way you want to play it. I'll be in touch and we'll take it from there,' Killian assured him and finished his drink. 'I'll have to give you a timescale though,' the wizard remembered.

'Telling when it's going to happen is fine. I need to know that,' Zoot reassured his friend.

'It's taking place tomorrow at midnight. The place —'

Zoot raised his hand. 'I'll stop you there

Killian. I don't need to know where it is right now. You can just take me there,' Zoot said simply.

'Yeah, okay,' Killian agreed and then he leaned forwards to shake Zoot's hand, but he knew what was coming. He received a huge hug from his friend.

'Before you head back, I would like to show you something,' Zoot said and peered into Killian's eyes.

'Okay,' Killian responded with curiosity.

'Follow me,' Zoot instructed and walked out of the room with the wizard following closely behind. Killian was intrigued, as he'd never gone any further than the living room and a small bathroom right next to it. Zoot took him down a long, white corridor and there was a large door at the end. The monk slipped his hand into his robe and produced a golden key. He twisted the lock with it and the door opened. Inside was a large, white room, not unlike the rest of the building. There wasn't much in there apart from a pedestal at the centre and a box set on top. The box was made of wood with beautifully crafted gold-leaf patterns. There was no lock or any indication of a dovetail joint or seam. Killian said nothing and waited for Zoot to make the next move. He stood next to it and closed his eyes and waved his hand over the box. There was a click and the lid slowly popped up. Zoot reached forward and lifted it the rest of the way.

'Killian,' Zoot said and gestured for him to look inside. Killian tentatively peered over the rim and was overwhelmed at the sight that greeted him. He gazed in silence for what seemed like only moments until Zoot closed the lid. Killian gave a heavy sigh as if he wanted to stay there forever. 'Tell no one,' Zoot insisted, eyes wide and serious. Killian didn't answer and just nodded. They left the room and didn't speak of it again.

Zoot followed Killian outside and watched him step off the porch and start up his bike. He put on his helmet and lifted the visor.

'You'll hear from me very soon,' Killian assured him. He pulled away and could still hear the jangling of chimes in the background. Added to the big smile on his face was also a warm feeling in the pit of his stomach. Zoot was a good ally to have. Killian already knew what they were up against, but he was more prepared for the situation to come. Relic could come back stronger this time. The force he had to deal with in the museum could be a lot more powerful on their second encounter. Killian had to work out what he needed to do to capture this thing and shut it down, so it couldn't return ever again. His life as a wizard was so easy... not.

Chapter 12
The Trap

Killian put his mobile phone back in his pocket after ringing his friend Zoot. Things had just got a whole lot easier with him on board. He drove back to the hills and Zoot's home. Once he'd collected him, they made their way to the end of town. Killian pulled up and parked his scooter on the top of an embankment, which overlooked Devil's Bridge. The night was drawing in. The grainy haze brought with it moisture, which dampened their clothes. It was a nice feeling after a particularly hot and dusty trip.

Zoot climbed off the back of the bike and felt stiff. He hated travelling on the scooter. He'd complained enough in the past for Killian to get a car, but the wizard refused.

'Did you enjoy the ride?' Killian joked, a wide smile lifting his face.

'Well, it was interesting,' he replied dismissively.

'No complaints?' Killian pressed.

'Nope,' Zoot replied as he wobbled on stiffened limbs.

'Thanks for coming along, Zoot, seriously,' Killian added.

'Anything to help an old friend,' Zoot replied coolly. 'If ever you're in trouble, you know I'll help if I can.'

'And vice versa,' Killian nodded. Zoot nodded back. 'I have to give you all the details now.' Killian looked at him. 'Is that okay?''

'Go ahead,' Zoot said, as he arched his back for some relief.

'It's going to appear right there at midnight.' Killian pointed to the underside of the bridge.

'What name has it taken?' Zoot asked. Now he was at the scene he needed more information.

'Oh yeah,' Killian said, 'Relic. That's what it said to me before it tried to force itself into my throat,' Killian answered and shuddered.

'Not a nice experience then?' Zoot grinned.

'No, not so much,' the wizard responded.

'I've got to know exactly what is going on before I can prepare myself for this,' Zoot said. 'Now is the time to tell me everything you know about this creature.'

'No worries,' Killian said. 'It's going to appear at midnight, as I've said. I don't really know how it is going to manifest itself. It was already embedded in a human cocoon when I fought it. And it tried to take over my body by oozing vapour from its mouth into mine.' Killian gave another shudder. 'I need to hold it in a spell and send it back to where it came from—and keep it there,' Killian added.

'This isn't going to be that simple,' Zoot said. It's been beaten once before and won't want to fall for that again. Are you sure it's going to appear under the bridge?'

'I trust my source; it said it would appear there and I believe it,' Killian responded, with a stern look on his face.

'And last time it got away in a split second. Before you even had a chance to use a spell,' Zoot said. 'So we need to freeze it somehow, the instant it appears.'

'Yes,' Killian agreed, 'that's definitely what we need to do.'

'But I don't know how,' Zoot confessed. 'We'll only have a small window of opportunity.'

'Yep. I have a plan though,' Killian responded.

'Which is?' Zoot looked sceptical.

'I've been referencing my books most of the night and I think I've got the right spell for the job,' Killian said with confidence.

'You'll have to use some kind of quickening spell to hold it,' Zoot said, with head tilted.

'Don't worry. I'll be ready the moment it appears, while you do what you're going to do,' Killian said, with curiosity.

'So, I'm guessing we're going to lay in wait?'

Zoot said and looked at the bridge with admiration. Devil's Bridge was a huge stone-built structure and as the mist rolled in the outline became more prominent. The strings of glowing lights that draped along its length made it appear a lot longer. 'Oh, that is beautiful,' Zoot said, 'Never really took much notice before. Being on the other side of town and all.'

Killian looked up and rolled his shoulders. 'It's a bridge,' he said without much thought. 'Concrete, steel and lights.'

'It's a beautiful bridge,' Zoot snapped back. 'You should take more notice of the beauty that surrounds us.' Zoot looked seriously at Killian, who peered back, not knowing what to say.

'Oh. Okay, sorry,' Killian apologised. Then the wickedness came out in the monk and he laughed. Killian realised that he was winding him up and grimaced, which made Zoot laugh louder.

'Lighten up, Killian. It may never happen,' Zoot said, still giggling.

'Funny guy,' the wizard retorted. 'Come on, we've work to do.' They made their way along the side of the river and down the embankment. It was still a warmish night, but with the mist thickening, it was dark on the footpath. The lights from the bridge were lovely to look at but didn't throw much light down there. As they got closer to the underside, things didn't appear so appealing.

'Ugh. It smells of urine and I can't even describe the rest.' Zoot retched. Killian could see the creases in his face and he couldn't help but snigger. He looked like a pea that had been left in a steamer.

'I thought you said it was a "beautiful bridge", Zoot?' Killian said. 'A bit of piss won't hurt you. You've been in that house too long.'

Zoot gave him a look of contempt. 'Well, it doesn't feel so beautiful right now,' his monk friend replied, through gritted teeth.

'Stop complaining and let's get this done,' Killian said. He fumbled in his pocket and retrieved his wand. He lifted it up and a light beam appeared on the tip. The brightness hurt their eyes at first, but when they could focus, they saw the state of the underside of the arch. Killian, let out a big sigh. There was a lot of stuff to move out of the way.

'Doesn't anyone clean up around here?' Zoot complained. He liked things in a clean and orderly fashion. There were dirty objects piled up all around. On one side was a heap of soiled clothes — like a small mountain. Killian lifted his wand higher and could see a coffee table, which had only three legs. There was also the obligatory shopping trolley and it looked shiny in amongst the other stuff. There were also bags of rubbish — empty bottles of beer and wine, also greasy pizza boxes.

Some bottles of booze were still half-full with green liquid and even Killian didn't think it was alcohol inside. He screwed up his face and made a gagging sound. Beyond the trolley was a wall of stuff he couldn't make out in the denseness of the short tunnel.

Killian pulled the metal trolley out of the puddle it was partially immersed in and set it upright. The wheels were all on so he made a grab for the coffee table. He grimaced when he touched the slimy surface of the wood.

'Give me a hand, will you?' he said, straining with it. Zoot reluctantly waded in and helped him lift it up.

'What do you want with this stuff?' Zoot asked, looking bewildered.

'It's for my living room,' Killian replied sarcastically and smiled at his friend. 'I've always wanted a three-legged coffee table to go with my three-legged chairs,' he joked.

'Living...' Zoot was about to continue and stopped when he realised that Killian was winding him up.

'Just put it in the trolley,' he said. They dropped it in lengthways and the leg on the other end broke off, and then the table fitted inside the framework.

'Now what?' Zoot quizzed.

'Push...' They made a run for it and smashed

into the rest of the debris, making an open patch of ground. 'Now I can work,' Killian said.

'Oh, I see.' Zoot appeared impressed. 'Good man,' he remarked.

Killian didn't waste any more time and knelt down on the wet stony ground. He dug in his pocket for the vial with the black sediment, the one he'd filled from conjuring the cloud spirit in his secret room. Zoot was intrigued and looked on in anticipation. He was going to ask him what he was doing, but knew Killian needed total concentration. Killian also produced a lump of chalk, but not any old chalk. This one dated back over hundreds of years. Zoot stood back and didn't utter a word while the wizard did his stuff. Zoot loved the way in which Killian worked his craft. He was a truly gifted wizard and Zoot trusted him, and only him, to work with.

The wizard unscrewed the glass tube and tipped the contents into the air, holding up the wand. The black particles danced and swirled around as if being toyed with by the wind. The mass then settled on the ground in a perfect dot. This is what gave Killian the exact spot in which the creature would appear. He took the chalk and drew a large circle. He went over it a few times to make sure it was a solid and prominent white line. There must not be any chance of an escape through a small gap in the barrier, he knew. He went on to draw sixteen rectangular prongs at intermittent positions around the outside.

Zoot kept on looking, filled with wonder.

Killian drew each prong so that each of the shorter edges touched the circle. He filled in the triangles with the white chalk.

When he'd finished, he eased back on his haunches. He gave it a long hard stare before bending over it again and chanting something under his breath. When he was completely finished, he stopped and lifted himself back again. He said one last word and for a few seconds, the circle glowed a luminous cream colour and finally dulled.

'Right, that's it,' he said excitedly. 'I can do no more at this point.'

'Um... would you mind telling me what you've just done?' Zoot looked eager to understand.

'Well, I hoping to catch the entity inside the circle,' Killian explained.

'Yep, I got that,' Zoot nodded.

Killian continued. 'And the oblong shapes that connect to it are kind of like an anchor. When the power ring holds Relic, the anchors will make sure it can't pull away. It won't last long and by that time... we would have blasted him back to the land of the dead. Well, hopefully,' Killian explained. 'Does that make any sense?'

Zoot nodded his head in confirmation.

'Where do I come in with my skills?' Zoot was mystified.

Killian wanted Zoot for the particular skills that he held. 'I want you to fully replicate Relic. So when it's trying to work out what's happening, I'll have my chance to set my banishing spell in motion and send it back.' Killian was not fully convinced about the plan, but it was all he had. There again, Killian never felt totally confident with his powers, but he'd solved many things in the past.

'So what happens now?' Zoot probed.

'Now? Now we wait and hope this works,' Killian said as he got up.

'Seems like a simple enough plan,' Zoot said.

'Yeah, but simple plans can come unstuck,' Killian admitted. 'You've just got to make sure you can distract him long enough so that I can have that small amount of time I need. The spell I've chosen should send Relic back and seal up the fissure. Zoot nodded and blinked his eyes in agreement. 'Can you replicate him, do you think?'

'That won't be a problem,' Zoot assured the wizard.

'Then we're all set,' Killian said.

'Yep, I guess. I'm hungry though,' Zoot added.

'Fancy a sandwich?' Killian asked as he produced one from his jacket pocket.

Zoot gave a look of disgust. 'Are you for real? It stinks down here and you're going to have a picnic,' Zoot squirmed.

'We could die tonight,' Killian reminded him.

Zoot soon changed his refrain. 'Oh, go on then,' he relented. 'What you got?'

'Cheese and pickle,' Killian said with a grin and handed him one.

'Can we eat this on the bank at least?' Zoot said and gave him puppy dog eyes.

'Come on, you wimp,' Killian chuckled and put away his wand, and they made their way up the bank, where they found a clean spot and sat waiting for death. They munched away on their cheese and pickle sandwiches as if it was a summer's evening in the park and they didn't have a care in the world. Both of them had been in this kind of situation before and knew the risks involved.

'Good sandwich?' Killian asked with a mouthful of pickle.

'Yep. Good sandwich,' Zoot replied.

Chapter 13
Midnight

It was approaching the midnight hour. Killian could feel the magical adrenalin build in his veins and the thumping of his heart seemed to boom in his ears. He craned his neck and glanced over at Zoot who appeared quite calm. Zoot was sitting cross-legged on the damp, grassy embankment with a serene look on his face. Killian creased his forehead, narrowing his green eyes.

'Aren't you just a little nervous?' Killian asked as he shone his phone light in his direction.

'When things get scary, I'll become nervous,' Zoot responded, 'but not before then. I do get agitated though. There's plenty of time to get nervous later.'

'Why do you get agitated? I thought you were all zen-like?' Killian asked curiously.

'When some idiot shines a light in my eyes,' Zoot retorted.

'Ah. Sorry. Well, I'm bricking it and I don't mind telling you that—' Killian stopped talking and tensed. He and Zoot could hear the town clock in the distance as it struck twelve. He wished he were there right now because the clock was set atop the town hall, which wasn't far away from the Square Inn pub, and he could do with a pint about now. As the chimes clanged away. a stiff wind whipped up from out of nowhere and slashed across them like a blade. This was a sign.

'What's happening?' Zoot whispered.

'Shhh…' Killian hissed; his concentration levels were raised. He and Zoot quickly made their way down the banking to the bottom and along the embankment to the spot where he'd chalked the pattern. There was someone sat under the bridge downing a bottle of wine.

'Get out of here now,' Killian growled and the homeless guy got up and walked off.

'Bas-tard cops,' he slurred as he stumbled along the path. Soon the lights on the bridge flickered and one or two even popped. There was an odour in the air, like burnt plastic mixed with musky, damp rags. Besides the clock chimes in the background, Killian could swear he could hear what sounded like the shrieks of lost souls. There were weird, wailing and sombre sounds, which pulled at your nerves and made you feel sick to the stomach.

'Killian, speak to me.' Zoot now sounded agitated and as he said it, they noticed that the white chalk circle began to steadily glow.

Killian spoke. 'It's simple really. When the

entity is fully formed — if my calculations are right of course and it does indeed appear inside the circle — then all I have to do is touch the chalk with the tip of my wand to seal it in. Once that happens it can't escape,' Killian explained. It all sounded too easy as far as Zoot was concerned.

'What if it doesn't land in the circle?' the monk asked. There *was* that particular problem.

'Mmmm,' the wizard replied.

'That doesn't fill me with confidence, Killian,' Zoot said.

'I've got the essence in the centre of the circle and that should pull it there,' Killian explained.

'Let's hope it does,' Zoot said.

'We have to take it as it comes,' Killian said. 'I'll deal with things as they unfold. Now, shush I need to concentrate.'

The wind suddenly picked up intensity and more bulbs brightened and popped on the bridge. Killian could feel the hairs stiffen on the back of his neck. He swallowed hard and ran his tongue around in his mouth. It had the atmosphere of a tropical storm approaching. The clouds above the bridge were whipping up into swirl patterns and the wind fanned the grassy embankment.

'I can feel it,' Zoot announced. 'Boy, this is nothing like I've encountered before,' he gasped.

'Okay, Zoot,' Killian spoke up in the heightening winds. 'When I touch the circle — you do your thing and try to confuse it. If I can keep the entity inside the confines of the spell, then maybe you can keep it occupied too, so that I can set another spell into place—to send it back,' Killian shouted. The whistling wind made it hard to make his voice heard.

The chalk circle became so bright that it lit up the entire underside of the bridge. The heat it produced lifted the intensity of the already hot weather. The wizard stood poised with wand in hand—the tip of which was glowing with energy. Killian's brown, wavy hair was plastered to his face and his jacket flapped like a cloak. Soon the debris from around them danced and floated to the same tune. It was as if there was a mini whirlwind under the bridge with papers, cartons and other debris obscuring his view.

'Keep your eyes peeled,' Killian screamed to Zoot. From within the white ring of smoke it emerged and only appeared as fumes at first. It materialised like the vapour from petrol. The almost purple mist seemed to claw its way from the ground upwards in long, finger-like tendrils. Killian's heart thumped heavily in his chest and he could feel every nerve-ending strain, as he waited for just the right moment to attack. His breath came in short, sharp puffs. Zoot peered intently at the strange smoke forming under the arch and twisted his neck towards Killian. The wizard's face was deathly white from the brilliance of the lighting field. His eyes were wide, almost bulging from their sockets. He was also trembling — Zoot could see his wand vibrating in his hand. The monk concentrated deep within himself and waited for just the right moment. The atmosphere was electric — sparks and long, lighted trails of energy cut across the underside of the bridge. You could hear, feel, smell the forces coming from inside the circle. The wind heightened and the chalky-circle became a blazing, ring of white.

Soon Relic began to manifest itself as a blackened mass of glistening goo. The wispy tendrils clawed its way from the ground — twisting and moulding itself into the shape of a human body. It morphed into a Grim Reaper type figure, tall, slim and completely enveloped in black. The silhouette emerged, taller than Killian. The wizard was poised, sweat, pouring down his glossy face, hands clammy and slick. He was close to the point of touching the chalk with his wand. Devilishly red eyes glowed from the newly formed head of Relic. And its arms began to form and stretch out at its shoulders. It was almost fully transformed and at the point of attack.

Killian swallowed hard, still directing the tip of his wand at the edge of the circle. He was shaking so much that the tip made light circles in the air. Just as Relic was only seconds away from solid form, something strange happened. From behind the apparition came *another* figure. It appeared to be that of a man and he was shouting something and waving his arms. Killian was momentarily distracted and that was enough to set hell loose.

'What the fuck...' Killian shrieked. He didn't or couldn't understand what was happening. Where did this guy come from? He wasn't there earlier, he was sure of it.

'Get away from my home you fucking bastards, get away from my fucking home,' the man yelled. And before Killian had a chance to warn the guy... he stepped right *through* the fully formed silhouette of Relic. What happened next was quick, deadly and totally out of Killian and Zoot's control.

The stranger had stepped over the white line, half in and half out of the circle. Once this happened, he was forcibly lifted off the ground and Relic fast disappeared into his mouth. When that happened, he immediately changed and Relic was fully immersed into him. Still three feet off the ground, the man's whole persona altered. He stiffened and raised his head. His eyes were pools of red. He lifted his arms and energy crackled through his limbs. He pointed his fingers and fired electrical charges at the wizard and the monk.

The white bolts of energy hit both of them

simultaneously and blasted them off their feet. They didn't have time to react as they tumbled onto the ground. By the time they'd recovered… Relic was gone. The underside of the bridge was in complete darkness as if nothing had happened. The last of the debris floated to the ground.

'Shit,' Killian rasped. 'Come on, Zoot, we have to get after him.' Killian winced. Holding his chest, he could still feel the heat from the blast on his clothes.

'Boy, that was powerful.' Zoot was still gasping for air. 'It's free now.'

'I know and we haven't time to discuss this. There look, he's heading towards the town,' Killian shouted and jabbed a finger at the suspended body that was floating in the direction of Windy Vale. 'We have to stop him before he gets there.' Killian scrambled up the damp embankment and leaped on his scooter. Zoot wasn't far behind and jumped on the back. They sped along the narrow, grassy trail and onto the bridge. Soon they were heading towards town too.

The dim headlight of Killian's scooter, only just about managed to pick up Relic's new host, floating away in the distance. Warm air blasted Killian's face as he hit fifty miles per hour at full throttle. Zoot gripped onto his waist and peered over his shoulder.

'Get me as close as you can and I'll figure out

a way of distracting it,' Zoot shouted in Killian's ear.

'I don't know what you've got planned, but we have to do something right now,' Killian screeched, trying to keep the bike straight and his eye on the movement ahead. The wizard was gaining on his target. Either Relic couldn't move any faster as an entity inside a human body, or it didn't care who or what was chasing him. Killian could feel he was getting closer. His hands tightened around the handlebars and he leaned his body forward, every muscle and sinew straining.

Killian got the bike within three metres of the entity. He slipped his left hand inside his jacket pocket and tried to keep the bike steady with his right hand. The engine buzzed loudly and at the very moment that he grabbed the wand, he hit a pothole. The scooter nearly toppled over and zigged and zagged all over the road. Luckily, Zoot managed to reach over Killian's shoulder and grab the handlebar with his left hand. They both jiggled the steering back on course. Killian passed his wand from his left hand to his right. He then steadied the Vespa with his left again and pointed the wand straight at Relic. He quickly uttered a spell and a blast of magical, white energy burst from the tip. It cut a big hole through the middle of the old man's body, sending blood and gore into the night air. Speckles of body fluid and gunk spattered the bike and Killian's face.

'Oh, that's fucking rancid,' Killian howled wiping his face with the back of his sleeve. Relic let out a humongous squeal that ripped across the sky. Killian knew he'd hurt it. The demon recovered quickly and picked up more speed, even though there were only two thirds of the body left. It looked disgusting as bits were still falling off. Relic, though, still kept control, but now it needed another host, sooner rather than later, or that body would be of no use and the spirit would die.

'He's looking for another victim to host. He can't stay in that form for too much longer. We have to stop him before he does,' Killian screamed, his voice swallowed up by the gusty wind and rattle of the engine. 'Zoot… Zoot?' Killian's bike suddenly felt lighter and he too could pick up speed. He then looked up when he heard the flapping of wings. There, above his head, was a huge griffin swooping towards Relic. Its wingspan was immense, covering at least six metres. It had a huge head with big, dark eyes and a deadly looking, hooked beak. The body was like a long barrel and the talons, which jutted out from its claws, resembled daggers. Killian beamed a huge smile. This was the power that the monk possessed. 'Go Zoot, go!' he cried and watched as the gigantic, mythical bird flew after the phantom demon. Killian, in his heart of hearts, hoped that

Relic could be stopped before he entered the town. It would be a lot more difficult and any number of people could get hurt along the way, if Zoot couldn't stop him.

'Attack, attack, attack!' Killian screamed. He sped along the road, his scooter at full speed.

Chapter 14
Griffin

Killian was always amazed at what Zoot could transform into. He wasn't a serene monk any more. Now, the sky was filled with the piercing screech of a giant bird. The night sky was a silhouette of the bird's form. Lucky for them, it was late and the roads were quiet and empty.

Killian was so engulfed in the spectacle flying over him that he almost crashed into a parked car and had to swerve to avoid it. He saw the majestic griffin swoop down in a wild attack, claws open and talons flexed. It let out a piercing screech and that was its biggest mistake. As the bird approached the floating body, Relic was ready and way too quick for him. The spirit demon conjured an invisible force, which it sent directly at the heart of the giant bird's body. It impacted the griffin in the chest area and sent it spiralling towards the ground. All Killian could do was watch as it crumpled and lost control.

'*Zoot!*' he screamed. The animal was stunned but began to recover from its free-fall, just before it hit the road. To Killian's relief it shook itself back into action and skimmed a parallel line along the surface and flew way off into the distance, back into the night sky. Killian twisted his neck and looked at the griffin swoop away into the black.

Killian thought deep inside that Zoot was gone for good. 'Damn, he must be injured. Fuck it, I'm on my own now,' Killian realised and turned back and sped on. How the hell am I going to do this alone? he pondered. Now with a heavy and sad feeling in his stomach, he concentrated on catching up with Relic.

The entity was getting closer to the town and Killian knew he had to do something fast. He was slightly out of range due to slowing down to see what had happened to Zoot, but he pointed his wand anyway. He concentrated all his wizard's power and was about to set another spell into motion, but stopped. The griffin came swooping in once more and had its talons outstretched like a giant grab machine. This time it got a lot closer and stealthily moved in undetected. Relic was unaware that he was about to be set upon. The bird flew low and at an angle under Relic's flank. It measured its pace and careered into the side of the demon's body. In one, short and lightning-fast manoeuvre, the griffin clamped onto its right arm and immediately flew away before Relic even realised it was there. As the bird creature retreated, it held in its talons the right arm of the victim. Relic screeched in agony once more as the pain tore through to its core. Killian physically heaved when he heard the snap. He saw the bird twist the arm and rip the limb straight from the shoulder — the sinews and muscle leaking red juice and skin flapping in the wind.

Killian felt a pang of sympathy for the poor guy that Relic was using as a shield. But Relic had to be stopped or there were going to be a lot more casualties. Zoot released the arm and tried another attack, but Relic was on to him and sent out an electrical charge in the shape of a rope lasso. It wrapped around the bird's throat and the demon yanked the bird out of the sky. The griffin smashed into the ground with a heavy impact and was pulled along by the ever-increasing power of the cable. Killian could see it choking the life out of his friend. The unconscious bird quickly morphed back into its original form, but was dragged along the ground like a water-skier leashed to a speedboat.

'*Zoot!*' Killian screamed and as quickly as he could, conjured a spell and fired it directly at the tether. The spell sliced through in an instant and Zoot tumbled helplessly along the roadside. Killian had to swerve heavily to avoid crashing into him. He thought he heard the sound of high-pitched laughter — was Relic mocking him?

Killian quickly abandoned his scooter and

rushed to his friend's side. Zoot wasn't moving and was lying in a crumpled mess on a patch of grass. The streetlamp lit his bleached and bloodied face, eyes closed. The wizard knelt over him. Panic set in and Killian didn't know what to do. This was his entire fault. 'I'm so sorry, Zoot. I never meant for this to happen,' he said, his voice distraught. 'What can I do to help you?' Killian sobbed.

Zoot moved slightly and opened his eyes. He let out a cough and groaned. Killian could see the agony in his eyes. It took some time but he eventually came round.

'I-I'm fine,' he said, but Killian knew he wasn't. 'You must go and stop that thing,' Zoot insisted. 'Honestly, I'll be okay. I've suffered worse. Go, Killian, please go and finish this,' Zoot said.

'I'll call an ambulance,' Killian said with concern and was about to ring from his mobile.

Zoot stopped him by grabbing his arm. 'No, only bumps and bruises, honestly. I know my own body. Go now, while it's still in a state of uncertainty,' Zoot said and sat up. He looked awful.

'Okay, if you're sure. I'll see you later, if... never mind,' Killian said and quickly made his way to the scooter. He lifted it off its side and set it upright. To his utter relief, when he turned the key, it started first time. He wasn't expecting that, especially as the fuel could have easily flooded the engine. He climbed on and shot down the road in the direction of the town. He couldn't see Relic any more, but he knew the spirit would be seeking another body to command right away.

The bright lights shone against the blackened sky of the early hour. The streets were deserted as he rolled into the centre of town. Ironically, the atmosphere was serene as if nothing was going on. Killian couldn't believe that the people were sleeping and right in their town was something deadly enough to kill everyone.

He came to a stop, rested his feet on the ground and steadied the bike. There wasn't much sound except for the purring of his engine and the buzz-buzz-buzz of a fluorescent light flickering away in the background.

'Where the hell have you gone?' Killian whispered. He could feel the heat from the engine rise between his legs. His clothes were soaked in sweat, mud and other disgusting bodily fluids from the dead body. 'If I ever get through this, I'm taking the longest shower ever,' he half-joked. This was going to be impossible, to track him on his own. Where would he start? Nothing was going on. He was in the middle of town on his own. 'You've got to be here somewhere,' he mumbled. He decided to take a different approach.

He calmed and stood upright using his

wizard's skills. He closed his eyes and meditated. There was nothing at first, but then he thought he could feel something. He opened his eyes again and a movement in the shadows caught his attention. It was only a glimpse at first in the corner of his eye. He turned immediately and saw a blackened, figure standing on the pavement opposite. It stood perfectly still, but with the streetlight shining behind it, it only gave the person a silhouette effect. Was this the new host Relic had acquired? Killian tensed and slowly fumbled for his wand, not taking his eyes from the person standing there opposite. The wizard lifted the wand out in front of him, the tip glowing white, crackling and spitting like a sparkler on bonfire night. Killian watched as the figure began to move and step off the pavement and onto the tarmac road. It was too dark to make out whether it was male or female at first. He swallowed but his mouth was so dry that nothing went down.

Killian studied how it moved and realised that it appeared be a female. Or it could have been someone with the light delicate stance of a woman.

'Stop right there,' Killian ordered, saying the words slowly. He gritted his teeth and gripped his wand so tightly that his knuckles whitened. There was a momentary pause… The figure did as was asked and stood in the middle of the road. It then spoke.

'Take it easy, Killian.' The soft voice spoke out. Then she continued to approach. Killian lifted his wand threateningly. 'Killian, it's me,' she said and he thought he recognised the voice but still wasn't sure.

'Stop,' he said again and she did. Whilst still holding his weapon out in front of him and not taking his eyes from the woman, he set the scooter on its stand. Once that was fixed, he stood next to it, the engine still ticking over.

'Come closer, but slowly. Who are you?' Killian demanded and when the figure stepped into the light, he saw right away.

'Killian, it's me,' the woman said. 'Cleo, Cleo Smoke.'

The warlock took a deep breath and studied the woman as she closed in. She could be possessed, but didn't appear to be a threat. But that's the way the entity would play it to gain Killian's confidence.

'Stop. How do I know you're not him?' the wizard repeated, still aiming his wand.

'Oh, I don't know, maybe because I don't have red eyes and reek of putrid death,' Cleo mocked.

He realised, as she got closer, that it was she. He relaxed a little and lowered his weapon. His whole body felt tired and he wanted to sleep but he knew he couldn't.

'What are you doing here, Cleo?' Killian

quizzed. She was within a couple of metres of him now and he could see her a lot more clearly. She was just as beautiful as the last time he'd seen her. This gave him new confidence and determination.

'I got this feeling that you may need my help,' she said. 'Well, do you?'

'I guess so, but I can't guarantee your safety. I've already got another friend of mine in a bad state. I don't want you to get hurt too,' he said honestly. 'Go while you can.'

'I'm not going anywhere. Don't you worry your pretty, little, head about me, Killian,' she said with a tinge of sarcasm. 'If this thing is allowed to roam in our world, then no one is safe. I've as much invested in this as you.'

Killian looked at her and she was right. She'd lost someone special due to this killing machine. It was as much her task as his. 'Okay, okay, but I've lost him,' Killian admitted and clenched his teeth in annoyance. 'He could be anywhere and inside anyone's body. I've partly failed already. I didn't want him endangering anybody else and now he's in this town doing just that. If it wasn't for that guy getting in the way…'

'What guy?' Cleo asked.

'Never mind, that's a story I'll have to tell you at a later time. We've got to find him right now,' Killian hissed.

'Well, lucky for you that I'm here now,' Cleo

said. 'He went that way.' She pointed in the direction of the main road through the town centre. 'What did you do to it? It looked like a slab of meat on two legs,' she explained. Killian winced and a stab of nerves gripped his insides. 'What is it?' Cleo pressed.

'There are a lot of people living there,' Killian sighed, 'as if we haven't enough to deal with.'

'We've got to stop it before it gets into a stronger body,' Cleo said and broke into a sprint. 'Come on, follow me,' she called back, her voice echoing in the distance. Killian got back on his scooter and followed in her wake.

Chapter 15
Windy Vale

Killian's scooter buzzed along on the uneven road at speed. The sound of his engine rattled through the stillness of the sleepy town. Windy Vale didn't cover a vast area but had many twisty roads leading to a network of streets. These narrow street areas ducked and dived in many directions, high and low. If you wanted to lose yourself there, then it would be really easy to slip out of sight. Killian had only moved there two years previous. As soon as he'd arrived, he liked the vibe of the place. The only problem was that he didn't have full knowledge of the area yet. He'd also lost sight of Cleo right away and that unnerved him. He looked hard but she was gone.

'Fuck,' he cursed, 'that's all I need.' Where the hell was she? And where did that freaky spirit go? He drove around for a while but came up with nothing. He came to a fork in the road, but his bike began to splutter and stopped. Killian looked at the gauge and shook his head—the tank was empty. How could he have been so stupid? He was in the middle of trying to save mankind and had forgotten all about fuel for his bike.

As luck would have it there was a twenty-four-hour petrol station a little way down the road. He pushed and freewheeled his bike down the hill and up onto the forecourt. It didn't take long to fill her up, but he had to use his debit card to pay at the pump. To his utter relief when he pressed in the button his scooter started right away.

'I love you, bike,' he whispered. That was his second piece of luck with his scooter that night. He ripped away from the garage and made it back to the fork in the road and planted his feet astride on the tarmac again.

There were shops and businesses in either direction and the buildings seemed to overhang as if squeezing him out. He scanned from side-to-side, probing, searching with deep concentration. The right-hand side sloped downhill, whilst the left side kept the same level. His stomach tightened when he thought he'd heard something. Was it a scream? He closed his eyes and strained his ears over the noise of the putt-putt of the engine and held his breath… There it was again, a voice that Killian couldn't quite make out. He wasn't sure where it was coming from, either. 'Come on, come on, Killian,' he said. 'People need your help.' He called on all his magical energy and realised that it was in fact to his left. He hoped he was right, because lives may depend on it, he thought.

'Left fork it is,' he said with confidence and snapped back the throttle. The bike pulled away with a mighty surge, screaming in its endeavour. Killian leaned over the handlebars and kept an eagle eye for his target. There was a small section of cobbled road and the bike vibrated its way over it. The bumpy surface jarred his chest and his bike bounced all over the surface. When he finally got back onto the smooth road again, he suddenly jammed on the brake. The front tyre dug in and the back lifted up off the ground and dropped back down with a couple of bounces. He kept his eyes peeled and could see a dark shape on the pavement ahead of him. He drove closer to it and could plainly make out that it was the homeless guy he'd been chasing all night. The body was in a hell of a state. with only one arm and a great, big hole in its midriff where its stomach had been ripped out. It was slumped on the pavement in a heap. Killian winced at the sight and felt guilty that it was his doing, but Relic had done the damage way before Killian had. He took one more look before he moved on and saw that the flies were having a real feast with the innards of the corpse. Killian couldn't look any more.

So, Relic had moved on, discarded the homeless guy and had taken up residence inside another poor soul.

'Jesus,' Killian sighed. Now the entity was going to be more difficult to find with a new human form. At least he knew what he was looking for before but now — he was at a loss. He pulled away from the corpse and moved further along. Then he saw something in the distance. It was slowly starting to get a little lighter, as dawn slowly approached. The situation would get easier with the light, but that meant everyone would be getting up for work. Relic would then have plenty of bodies to use and the witnesses would be a hundredfold. Killian saw straight away that it was Cleo Smoke standing in the middle of the road. hands raised, ready for a battle. Killian went steaming in and stopped next to her. He shut off the engine and steadied the bike on its stand. He sidled up close and could see that she was poised for action.

'What is it, Cleo?' Killian asked, slightly out of breath. 'I can't see anything,' he said as he looked all around, brow furrowed. 'What are you looking at?'

'Our friend is in that alleyway,' Cleo reported, not taking her eyes from the darkened corridor.

'Okay,' Killian said, staring in the same direction. It was semi-dark, but with a streetlamp casting a pale, yellow light over the entrance. 'When did you see it?'

'Only moments ago,' Cleo spoke slowly and

quietly. 'It discarded that body and I think, took on another.'

'I'm guessing there isn't an exit at the other end?' Killian said.

'I think so or it would have already disappeared,' Cleo said looking at Killian for a second and quickly refocusing on the lane.

'What are we dealing with here, Cleo? So Relic has claimed yet another poor soul,' Killian said, his voice filled with anguish.

'Yep, I'm afraid so.' Cleo's tone dropped, to match the sadness she felt.

'You saw it?' Killian said.

'Yep, another male,' she said.

'We can't let it get away this time,' Killian insisted. 'So we're in its way? It has to go through us. We can stop it this time, between us.'

'It hasn't worked so far.' She was right and Killian knew it. He lifted his wand and pointed it in the direction of the ally.

'How are we going to do this?' Cleo asked. 'What if I burst in there and you stand behind and blast him,' she reasoned.

'You can't just pile in there. He'll be waiting to tear you apart. You've seen what he can do. You'll be going in blind,' Killian responded. 'I'm not going to let that happen. He's already hurt my friend, Zoot.'

'What the fuck do we do then?' she hissed. She

was getting agitated.

'Hold on… let me think.' Killian looked around and knew that the light would come soon, which would work to their advantage because this thing didn't like the light. And there wasn't much cover, so when it did come out there was nowhere to hide.

'Killian. Well, have you got anything?' Cleo's impatience was bubbling.

'We draw him out,' Killian said sensibly. 'And once he's out in the open, we take him the fuck down.'

'How?' Cleo asked and stared at him with her crystal blue eyes narrowed.

'How about we just simply call him out?' Killian suggested.

It seemed plausible. Cleo looked at him incredulously. She mulled it over in her mind and shrugged her shoulders. 'Do you think he'll fall for that?' she responded. It did seem a stupid idea at first, but what did they have to lose? 'Okay. I'm good with that.'

'There's only one way to find out if it'll work,' Killian said and shouted from the street, '*Relic*! *Relic*, there's no escape. You may as well come out, mate. Time is running out for you. It's getting light, my friend, and we know that you don't like the day time.' They waited for a response, but nothing happened.

Cleo squinted at Killian and shook her head. 'Well, that didn't work,' she said, the sarcasm dripping from every word.

'Shut up, Cleo. *Relic!*' Killian repeated in a much higher tone. 'Come on out. You're surrounded. I'm getting a bit pissed off now.'

Cleo looked at Killian again and was confused. 'There's only the two of us Killian,' she remarked.

'I know that, but he doesn't, does he? It's called a bluff, Cleo,' Killian said. 'Haven't you ever heard of... aw, do you know what... just forget it.' Killian carried on. 'If you don't come out, then we're coming in,' he said. 'Now get ready for anything, Cleo.'

They waited and stared into the block of darkness at the end of the alley. There was some movement, then the sound of someone whimpering, which sounded like a woman's voice. Killian and Cleo were confused.

'That doesn't sound good,' Cleo said.

'I thought you said that it had taken over a man's body?' Killian said. 'That doesn't sound like a man,' he added. 'Oh Jesus, I hope he hasn't got someone else in there.'

'I'm sure it was... a milkman, I think,' she said.

Well, that made sense, Killian thought. A milkman would be delivering in these early hours. And when he looked around there was a milk float parked a bit further up the street. So why could he hear a woman's voice? He must have taken a hostage, he pondered. That would make things really tricky.

'Come on out, right n —' Killian stopped when he saw something moving within the shadows. The sound of a muffled voice grew louder. Cleo and Killian stood in the middle of the street, Cleo Smoke with arms raised and Killian with his wand trained on the darkness. They waited… poised. There was a shuffling sound and then some more movement.

Firstly, a man appeared, slowly making his way into the streetlight. He was dressed in a blue jacket, and light-blue work trousers. Must obviously be the milkman, Killian assumed. Cleo tensed and Killian gave her a quick glance and shook his head, not to attack. The milkman's right arm was outstretched and another figure emerged from within the darkness; it was indeed a woman. Relic did have a hostage in there. This spirit was getting sneaky. The woman was slight and dressed in a pink dressing gown and slippers. The milkman had his hand around her mouth and her eyes blazed wildly in terror. Her legs were buckled under as the milkman dragged her out. She was trying to kick and scream her way out of a bad situation, but Relic had her tightly gripped. Both Cleo and Killian could tell that she was terrified.

'How did he get her?' Cleo hissed.

'I don't know, but he has. She must have been disturbed by the commotion outside her house,' Killian assumed. 'Oh shit,' he said and stopped talking.

'Oh, shit what?' Cleo pressed. 'Killian. Snap out of it.'

Killian recognised the woman right away — it was Penny White. The wizard's mouth dropped open. He couldn't believe what was happening. Cleo realised that he recognised the girl and tried to get his attention.

'Killian. Killian. Who is she?' Cleo asked urgently. 'Do you know her? Tell me. Who is she?' Cleo repeated.

Killian was zoned out for a moment and then collected his thoughts. 'Oh, I'm sorry. It's Police Chief Hathaway's personal assistant,' he said. 'Her name is Penny White.'

'You do know her then?' Cleo quizzed. 'How on earth do you know a mortal?'

'Well, only briefly. She's the contact I was telling you about,' Killian gasped.

'And now she's a hostage!' Cleo said with a huge sigh. 'This is going to end badly.'

Chapter 16
Hostage

The last of the darkness was slowly fading as the dawn began to make its appearance, giving a fresh brightness that made everything real. The milkman stood bolt upright, unnatural and deathly. His eyes glistened with a bloody stare that shook Killian to the core. He wasn't a man any more — his skin was already mottled, just like the others. It was too late for him but there was still time for Penny. She was petrified, her eyes wide and glistening, her brow furrowed and teeth clenched. Killian felt a pang of terrible guilt. If he'd sorted this under the bridge then no one would have been hurt. And now someone he'd only just met, someone he already felt something for was in the middle of everything. She was only seconds away from death and he could do nothing to prevent it.

She whimpered, her head tilted to one side where the ghoul clearly had her hair gripped. He yanked her head and she let out a laboured screech. Her cheeks glinted as the tears flowed. Killian could see that she was dressed only in a silky, wrap-around dressing gown. Her black hair was dishevelled where normally it would be perfectly groomed. She'd obviously been woken by the commotion and got out of bed to see what was happening outside and that was her big mistake. His stomach jolted at the thought of her being hurt.

He could see her body clearly outlined through the sheer material of the nightwear. He lifted his eyes to meet hers and he swallowed hard in his throat. She was sobbing, but there was something else. Killian looked on helplessly. She was also slowly falling into a trance. Her eyes began to glaze over and her whole body stiffened. She was being taken over and he couldn't let that happen. He couldn't let her life force drained away, right in front of him. He had to act fast or it would be too late.

'Killian, what do we do?' Cleo snapped him back to reality.

'Relic, let her go,' Killian calmly insisted.

The spirit just laughed a deep, curdling cackle, which vibrated the very ground they stood on. 'She is mine now, as is everything in this world.' Relic spoke through the mouth of the dead milkman. Its eerie smile and deathly eyes cut Killian to the quick. Killian's memory was immediately taken right back to his very first encounter with the beast, when they wrestled on the floor of the museum. He could literally smell its rank breath and could still see its yellowed, cracked teeth and those disgusting, rotting gums. Then he thought of the poor, innocent milkman going about his daily task. He didn't want or expect any of this, but he was no more. Killian couldn't think of any of that any more. He still had the power to help someone and that was Penny. So he had to push all his magical energies into that task. He needed to stall him. He needed time to formulate a plan and stop the entity where he was standing, and hopefully release Penny in the process.

'You can't stay here, Relic. This is not your world. Let the woman go and you can return there,' Killian urged. 'I can help you. I can give you what you want,' he said stalling for time. Cleo Smoke looked at him incredulously but stayed silent. As the first strands of the morning light emerged, Killian noticed a flicker in the demon's eyes. He knew the demon would soon be at its weakest in the daylight. It would still hold power, but wouldn't be as strong in natural light. They had an advantage over him at last and he knew it. For the first time since the sorcerer encountered this being, he felt confident.

'You are trying to trick me, wizard,' Relic said with penetrating, bloodshot eyes. 'If you and the shadow nymph attack me, you'll end up killing her.' Relic sneered and looked at his traumatised captive. He yanked at her head and it snapped back. Penny didn't make a sound as if lost inside her own world. Killian managed to hold himself back but flinched. Relic noticed this and chuckled. 'You're not going to stop me and chance her getting hurt. You have feelings for this... woman,' Relic continued and suddenly began to move away.

'Killian, where's he going? We have to do something,' Cleo hissed and shuffled in her position. 'We can't let him get away. Killian...'

'Stop right there,' Killian growled, but the spirit was dragging the girl along with him.

'He's getting away,' Cleo hissed.

Killian quickly looked in the direction Relic was dragging his victim and soon realised that he was going towards Windy Vale Castle. The wizard physically winced.

'Oh shit, no,' Cleo cursed and looked mortified. 'If it enters there —'

'I know,' Killian cut her off. But he knew as much as Cleo that it made Penny's rescue plan a whole lot harder. Castles, more than anywhere, held the remnants of the dead — ghouls, ghosts and spirits, you name — Relic knew that too.

'We've got to stop him. Once he's on the ground, who knows what will happen?' Cleo snarled. She was right, but how could they attack

Relic without hurting Penny?

'I know, I know,' Killian repeated, but Relic held all the cards. It was too late now anyway — Relic had already entered the castle grounds. This wasn't good. This wasn't good at all. Cleo and Killian followed slowly behind the demon. The boundary line was a thin layer of stones set in the ruins of the grounds — a faint portrayal of the original protection of the castle wall. They stopped and stared at the fast-disappearing devil spirit.

Killian and Cleo quickly and reluctantly stepped over the threshold. They felt a shiver of evil shoot right through them. They were now in the dark and deadly world, which had been waiting for eternity. Killian swallowed and sucked in a breath.

'There's no going back now, Cleo,' Killian remarked.

trembled. Nothing much ever scared her. But they were on their own with the most powerful entity they'd ever encountered and the added fate of the dead.

'We haven't only got Relic to worry about now,' Cleo winced. 'The world of the dead awaits.'

'If I can get Relic to let Penny go, then maybe we can open a rift and send him back before too many of the dead appear. That's all I've got,' Killian admitted and didn't sound confident, but the light was draining Relic's strength. They had to confront him now, out in the open. If he moved into the depths of the dungeons, then that was it. 'Cleo, get around him and cut him off,' Killian insisted. She did as she was asked and swooped at great speed.

'Stop right there, Relic,' Cleo said and blocked his way. She was stood with arms raised and a look of deadly determination on her face.

'Get out of my way, shadow nymph, while you still can,' Relic growled.

'Don't let him pass you,' Killian called out. Cleo used her invisible force field to push against the demon. But Relic quickly shot back a burst of energy that sent her sprawling across the courtyard. She tumbled over, but spectacularly flipped into an upright position before she hit a brick pedestal. Killian was impressed.

'You'll have to do better than that, scumbag,' she called back smugly.

Before Relic could mount a second attack, he was smashed from behind by the huge impact of supernatural force from the wizard. Caught completely off guard, the demon lost hold of its hostage and Penny fell loosely from its grip. She tumbled in a half-unconscious state down a grassy banking. Killian looked on helplessly as she rolled off a stone ledge and landed with a sickening thud, cracking her head against a cast-iron statue of a knight.

'Oh shit, Penny. I'm sorry, I'm sorry!' he shouted after her, but he couldn't help her now. It was his magical force that had caused it and if she died, then it was his doing. He had to push that to one side and stop Relic right now, while he still had the chance. He instantly refocused and pushed all his energy into finishing Relic. Penny would have to wait.

The beast got back up on its feet, but with the hostage gone and its powers partially drained — it was at its most vulnerable. Neither Killian nor Cleo was about to give it time to refocus so they attacked instantly. Cleo let rip with a powerful barrage of black energy, which forced it against the great stonewall of the inner castle. Relic was pinned and tried to fight it, but its energy was dwindling fast. Killian immediately shot a burst of magical power from his wand, which tore the man in half and finally released the spirit from inside. The limp body fell to the ground in two pieces — his inners spilt out in a mess of blood and gore, which pooled in the middle of the green manicured lawn. In its place was Relic's true form, a great, blackened cloud of energy and evil. Inside its canopy were flashes of white lightning and the unearthly, shrieks of the dead. Relic rose quickly like a forest fire.

Killian urgently called to Cleo. 'Use your power to contain it, Cleo… Now!' Killian bellowed, his eyes fiery and face stern. 'You have to capture it for me to send it back.'

Cleo immediately and skilfully whipped up a cloudy, blackened sphere and set it around the fast-forming energy of the spirit jumper.

She quickly engulfed the spirit inside a rounded, black ball. Her face was a world of concentration, her arms held out in front of her as if sleepwalking. Cleo's powerful energy sealed Relic inside a huge, energy bubble. She could see it trying to fight back. Relic desperately tried to find a way through the barrier, but Cleo held fast. The spirit jumper was clearly weakening and for the first time since its encounter with Killian, looked at its most vulnerable. Now was the time to strike.

'I won't be able to keep it in there for long,' she shrieked, the strain already showing on her face. 'It's way too strong, Killian. I need you to do something now!' Her arms were shaking and the skin on her face taut.

'I won't need long to do this. Hold it for as long as you can,' Killian said as he focused, blocking everything out from his thoughts. He had to be at one with Relic and that was going to be scary. But things were happening…

Suddenly, unbeknown to the wizard, beings began to appear around them. The dead had been aroused and were coming to see what had breached their ground. They swarmed from below like sewerage, seeping, sludge through a storm drain. With the lifting of the lost souls came a terrible chorus of sombre moans.

Killian worked on conjuring the spell that would open a tear in the fabric of this world and the other and send Relic back. But now there were hundreds of ghosts emerging from everywhere. Killian's supernatural instincts warned him that he was in danger, but he couldn't veer away from the job at hand. Cleo strained under the enormous pressure of Relic, who was squirming and pressing against her powers. Its deadly forces were weaker, but it was still strong and made it as difficult as it possibly could. Even Relic could see the dead rise and knew that their distraction would be all he needed to break away from the wizard and shadow nymph.

The dead were closing in. Those poor, lost souls needed to feast on the living too, but that was all about to change.

Chapter 17
A Wizard's Best Friend

As Killian sat down and closed his eyes in concentration, he blotted out the deadly, dangers that were approaching. He blotted out the wild protests of Cleo Smoke, who he could barely hear – screaming in the depths of his consciousness. She needed him but he just couldn't help her at this very crucial time. He even, although his heart was aching, pushed to one side the image of the unconscious body of Penny White.

But he could also feel something new and dangerous bleeding into the outer edges of his psyche, but he needed to do this one task and he would have to deal with all that later. So he dug deep into his magic. He hadn't visited this level of concentration in hundreds of years. It was tranquil and scary and he knew that Relic would soon appear and Killian would need everything he had to fight.

As Killian zoned out and all hell broke loose inside the confines of the castle grounds – something appeared in the distant sky. Through the haze of grey morning clouds, a speck emerged. As it approached, its form got bigger and bigger until it fully engulfed the sky above the turrets of the medieval castle. The dragon was quite beautiful but also brought with it a deadly message. Its outer skin was semi-transparent against the bland, dawn sky so that no mortal could see it or report its flight. The dragon's huge wingspan was easily twelve metres across with a long, thick tail that tapered off to a point. Its eyes were like huge, glassy dinner plates and when it opened its mouth it revealed layer upon layer of jagged teeth. The creature was barely making a sound as it glided across the expanse. It peered down and saw the army of the dead rise— emerging from the depths. The dragon also realised the imminent danger that the wizard and the shadow nymph were in. There was also a female body down there, still and helpless. If she was alive or dead, he didn't know, but what he did know was that she was in immediate danger. The rising souls of the dead were closing in.

Urgently Zoot swooped down at great speed, like a missile, flapping his huge wings and not making even the smallest of sounds. Unaware of their impending doom, the hordes of ghosts continued on their quest towards the wizard and driven by an unworldly desire to overcome and destroy him. The dragon soon spotted the black mass, which was Relic's form. Although entrapped by the shadow nymph, it could still use its dark powers to control the creatures around them. All it needed to do was to distract Killian Spooks for a short while so that it could escape the clutches of Cleo Smoke. Zoot wasn't about to let that happen.

The dragon swooped high into the sky and whipped around in a long arc. It slowed its pace and dropped down low, lining up its targets. It levelled off until it was parallel to the ground, but high enough for the enemy not to suspect what was going to happen next. The medieval battleground was about to see an attack that would be more deadly than any of the mortal battles it had encountered through its entire history. The dragon steadied itself and opened its wide jaws. Soon, a blue fire smouldered deep within its stomach. The flames swirled around like a hurricane in the pit of its belly. The furnace began to rise from the depths and funnel its way to the base of the giant bird's throat. Nothing could stop it now.

The black dragon glided along in a smooth flight and exploded a long belch of yellow fire from its open mouth. The scorching trail blazed the length of the castle grounds. In one, long exhale of breath, the deadly attack viciously cut down the masses like a Samurai sword slicing through a ripened melon. Soon, the dead were exploding all around in wild flames and billowing, choking smoke. Their deafening shrieks and howls could only be heard in the confines of the ancient grounds, where they were laid to rest once more.

Most of the wakened souls were so engrossed in the hypnotic power that Relic had over them, that they didn't even see the devastation that was happening all around them. There were, however, some who did pick up on the attack. They tried to fight back with the puny weapons that were buried with them when they died. Even they didn't have enough time to alert the others to the impending doom. Some tried to scatter like ants, but there was nowhere to hide. The dragon, after the first wave, flew back up into the sky. It then turned for another devastating encounter. It came in fast, belching fiery, yellow flames, blanketing the ground, seeking out all those who tried to hide, and blasting them to oblivion. The wails of the dead echoed throughout the battlefield, in a pitiful and sombre chorus until almost all perished.

Cleo Smoke, still holding Relic in her grasp, lifted her level of power, now that she realised there was a dragon was helping them.

Finally, after wave upon wave of attacks, Zoot took one last flight until he was satisfied that Killian and the rest were safe. His work was done. The dragon eventually withdrew and swooped high up over the castle and disappeared behind the treeline. Once the beast settled on the ground, its breathing slowed and calmness prevailed. Soon the magnificent form of the mythical creature began to change. It quickly reduced in size, but gently and in many stages. Gone now were the slick, black scales and disc-like eyes. The long, curved talons receded and finally took on the shape of human feet. The huge wings shrank back into the familiar limbs of the monk. Until, finally, he morphed back into his usual human persona once again. He fell to the ground in an exhausted state. He was bruised and cut but, unbelievably, there were no broken bones. Everything ached, but that was nothing. He had helped his friend, Killian, and now it was up to the wizard to finally put an end to the existence of Relic. So Zoot gathered what little strength he had left and got up. He made his way towards the castle so that he could stand beside his wizard friend.

***

Visions flashed through the wizard's mind — visions of a huge, mythical dragon. He smiled, knowing that his friend Zoot hadn't let him down. He also knew that the monk would try and keep his friends safe as well. It was Killian's turn to end this now.

He raised his right hand, firmly gripping the wand — like a music conductor about to address his orchestra. Soon the tip exploded into life, unleashing a bright, magical beam of light. The sorcerer swirled his wand around and around in a small, white circle. like a sparkler on bonfire night. He began at waist height and then he teased it into a much bigger ring. The wider he drew the ring — the bigger it became. Soon it swirled into a mighty whirlpool of solid light. This was so powerful that not many could resist it.

The energy it produced sucked at the immortal. Soon any strays that hadn't been consumed by the mighty dragon were sucked deep into the swirling void. Things became clearer and Killian could now see Cleo struggling to hold onto the demon spirit. It wouldn't be long before Relic was free again to unleash evil. Killian breathed deeply and worked his magic. Cleo screamed as Relic began to slowly break through her force field.

'I can't hold it, Killian,' she screamed. 'It's breaking through.' Within seconds the phantom was finally free. Its colossal strength blasted the shadow nymph through the air and across the courtyard. Cleo tumbled to the ground and landed with a thud against the castle wall. She fell silent.

Killian was alone now in his fight to contain and try and banish the spirit jumper. Relic was once again focused on finding another body. It didn't have to be perfect — it just needed a vessel. It spotted Penny on the ground and was about to swoop down and devour her. It tried to move but felt something pulling it away from its natural course. Relic was intrigued when it realised that it was being sucked into the vortex. The wizard's magic was powerful, but Relic had other ideas. It was close to full daylight and Relic was weakening by the second. He stared at Killian with hypnotic, red eyes.

'You think you can destroy me, wizard? You think you are more powerful than I?' the entity bellowed, but it knew that's exactly what Killian was doing. Relic gave an almighty roar and pulled away from the ever-beckoning ring of light. Killian stayed strong and concentrated his mind, as he'd never done so before. 'Let me be, wizard, before I destroy you,' Relic bluffed. Killian could suddenly feel Relic gaining supernatural energy from the remaining ghosts of the castle. He could feel it sucking energy from all around the walls and in the ground. Killian could also feel its power getting a little stronger. This frightened the wizard and for a moment began to second-guess himself. Did he have enough power to do this? He had too. So he drew on everything he had to keep the monster in his grasp.

Relic let out a huge belly laugh from deep

within its smoke-filled plumes. It pulled away with all its might and could feel Killian weakening. The wizard was having trouble keeping hold — beads of sweat dripped down his brow. He took in a huge lungful of air, his hands trembling. He still held fast and slowly gained control again, pulling the spirit back into the void.

'Let me fucking go, wizard,' Relic bellowed and ranted, knowing that it was losing this battle. Killian closed his eyes and a smile masked the strain he felt. This gave him a whole new level of power and he stood taller.

'*Porfotulas Emondos*,' Killian screamed, which seemed to tear at the black fog and reel the monster in towards the ring with a colossal suction. Relic's black tendrils swirled on the edge of the whirlpool as ghostly bodies flew past the wizard and were catapulted to the depths of the void. Killian held on as Relic was teetering on the rim. Its black mass slowly disappeared like water down a plughole. When he saw this happening, Killian swirled the wand at a mighty rate.

'Die, you bastard, die,' he screamed and soon the colossal power of the warlock was way too much and the phantom that was Relic… was finally ripped from this world and disappeared into the ether… its final shrieks echoed in the distance… it was gone.

Killian instantly fell back and tumbled onto

the ground. He was exhausted and drained of magical energy. He lay there for a few moments, his stomach heaving and contracting, gasping for air. He eventually opened his eyes and shielded them with his hand, filtering out the brilliant, summer sun. He eased up onto his elbows, still breathing hard. The ground had a scorched spot in the shape of a circle and Killian knew it was the mark of the demon. Relic was nowhere to been seen and the wizard let out a huge sigh. He swept his eyes over the grounds and everything was calm. His wand? He realised he didn't have his wand. He expressed a spell and sure enough, it flew through the air and landed in his hand. Then it hit him like a sledgehammer. Where were his friends, Cleo, Zoot, but most of all— where was Penny?

'Penny,' he gasped and he got up with urgency. Was she okay? He had to find her.

Chapter 18
Unconscious

Killian scuttled down the bank and saw Penny's body sprawled on the ground. He felt a rush of panic and his heart pounded. He could see her pink, silky wrap had tangled up under her back. She was lying in a weird position with her head tilted at an awkward angle. He could also make out a large cut on her right temple and blood congealing around it—a bruise already formed. Her right arm lay across her chest and her left was loosely set at her side. There was another bruise forming on her right leg, which was bent at the knee and leaned against the statue she'd struck, leaving her left leg outstretched on the grass. Killian could also see that the hem of her short, nightdress had fallen away, exposing her bare, slim thighs and perfectly trimmed, pubic hair. He quickly pulled down her nighty to save her embarrassment, but making sure that he didn't move her in case she'd broken or fractured something.

'Cleo, call an ambulance,' Killian shouted from below, the panic clear in his voice.

'Okay,' she called back but wasn't too thrilled to use her mobile. She saw something glinting in the grass and when she bent over to pick it up, saw that it was a mobile phone. She held it for a moment and the screen flashed into life. An image popped up of an attractive woman in her mid-forties, roughly the same age as the milkman. Cleo closed her eyes and a lump clogged her throat. She must be his wife, she thought, looking at the disgusting mess that once was the man himself. She quickly tapped in the number for the emergency services. She knew that if she'd used her phone the police would be able to trace everything back to her. 'Hello. Ambulance, please. There's been an accident. There's a woman unconscious in the grounds of the castle and a man's dead body here too.' As soon as she'd relayed the information, she hung up. She knew that the police would be informed right away and she didn't need the hassle. Straight after that, she could hear the sounds of the sirens echoing across the town. Killian took off his jacket and placed it over her cold body.

'Penny,' he whispered. 'Penny,' Killian repeated, but she didn't respond. He felt for her pulse with two fingers at the side of her neck. A smile lifted his face when he felt the thump-thump-thump gently reverberate through his fingertips. He closed his eyes and whispered,

'Thank God.' Even though he wasn't religious.

Cleo joined him at his side. 'Is she okay?'

Killian nodded. 'I think so, she has a pulse and she's breathing normally. Her head is another matter.' He looked worried. 'She had quite a knock on that statue,' Killian said, pointing to the metal frame of the figure. 'Cleo, you'll have to make yourself scarce,' he said. 'I'll make a statement to the police when they arrive,' he insisted.

'What about him?' Cleo asked, looking at the ridge of the bank. Killian followed her gaze. 'Who is he?' she pressed.

'Oh shit. That's Zoot—I'd forgotten about him,' Killian said and looked into Cleo's eyes. 'You know. The dragon.'

She thought for a moment. 'Oh. He's a shape shifter?' she realised, her eyes bright.

'Yep. Now you're getting there. And he happens to be a really good friend too,' Killian responded.

'He's not looking too good if you ask me,' Cleo said. Zoot was bashed about and unsteady on his feet.

'Do me a favour and check him out while I look after Penny.' Killian said. 'Can you ride a motor scooter?' He asked. Cleo nodded. 'Could you take him home and leave my bike there. I'll pop by later to see if he needs me.'

'Shouldn't he go to a hospital?' Cleo said with

concern.

'No. No, Zoot can take care of himself. If you get him home then he'll take it from there. That's what I would have done anyway,' Killian reassured her.

'Oh, okay, if you're sure?' she said, but was a little sceptical.

'Now go, quickly,' Killian insisted. 'There's going to be enough to deal with on my own without explaining why you two are here too. There's a dead man ripped in half on the castle grounds and a woman's unconscious body — in her nightclothes, too. Suffice to say, it doesn't look good. This is going to take some explaining to the authorities. But I do have a "Chief Card" that might be enough to get me out of trouble. I'll see you again sometime,' Killian added and touched her shoulder with affection. 'I hope this helps you a little with your grief. Relic is gone for good. Now go quickly.'

'Okay. I understand, Killian. Bye,' Cleo said and climbed back up the slope. Soon she and Zoot were on Killian's bike and he could hear them pull away in the background.

Not long after that, along with the ambulance, came two police cars with their full blues 'n' two's blasting away. Cleo had taken the back streets and missed them, Killian assumed. The area was soon set up as a crime scene. Penny was tended to, while

Killian was whisked away in one of the patrol cars — taken to the station for questioning. As he was being pushed into the police car, he could see a small gathering of people from the town. He could also hear whispers of the sighting of something that resembled a dragon, but no one could be sure. Killian gave himself a wry smile.

The warlock was questioned, but he called for Chief Inspector Hathaway to come in for a personal chat. When they met face to face for the very first time, there was an awkward conversation.

Hathaway finally gave the order for Killian to be released. He wasn't allowed to leave town or make a visit to the hospital where Penny was kept. It was all part of the investigation and he was still a suspect. Finally, the next morning, he got word from Hathaway that Penny had come round. The chief inspector also said that she had told him everything and that now he wasn't a suspect any more.

Hathaway also mentioned that Penny was asking to see him and that he was free to go to the hospital and see her. Killian's heart jumped at the fact that first, she was going to be okay and second, that she wanted to see him after all that had happened to her.

He nervously walked down the corridor of the hospital. Chief Inspector Hathaway had personally made sure that his assistant had a private room. Killian stopped by the door and paused. He nervously straightened his jacket and breathed into his hand to check his breath. He gave a little knock and walked inside.

Penny was awake and sitting up in bed. She beamed when Killian entered the room. She wore a blue and white hospital gown, which would have looked frumpy on anyone else, but on her, it looked good. Her head was bandaged from the top of her brow covering her dark locks. She didn't have make-up on, but that didn't matter. Her beauty shone through like a beacon.

'Hello, Mr Spooks,' she joked.

Killian shook his head. 'Penny, I think we've gone past that stage, haven't we?' he asked and handed her a punnet of mixed grapes.

'Only joking, Killian, oh thank you,' she said.

'I didn't know what else to bring,' he admitted.

'That's fine, I like grapes,' she said and peeled back the cellophane to sample one.

'I'm so sorry you were dragged into this,' Killian said honestly. 'How is that?' he said pointing to the swirl of a wrap-around bandage.

'Oh this,' she replied, touching it with her right hand. 'This is fine. I think it's coming off tomorrow. I hope so anyway,' she continued and gave a look as though she couldn't wait.

'So, you're going home tomorrow?' Killian

assumed.

'Yes, nothing is keeping me in here now,' she said with relief.

'How are you getting home?' Killian asked curiously.

'Hathaway is sending a car for me,' she said. 'Never mind that. What happened after I passed out? And who was that beautiful girl?' Penny asked and raised her right eyebrow.

'Oh uh, Cleo… Cleo Smoke,' Killian answered, but for some reason felt awkward saying it.

'She was stunning. Is she… your girlfriend?' Penny looked as if the answer couldn't come quick enough. Killian burst out into a loud belly laugh. Penny looked put out and her expression changed from warm to sullen. 'What's so funny?' she said angrily.

Killian realised he'd upset her and stopped. 'S-sorry,' he stumbled and looked a bit more serious. 'It's funny because I'm not her type,' he said. She looked confused and Killian understood that he hadn't made himself clear. 'Penny, she's not a threat,' Killian revealed.

At that, Penny did look annoyed as well. 'So you think I'm interested in you. You've got tabs on yourself, haven't you?' she exploded.

Killian didn't see that coming. It was meant to be a nice welcome and a calm, conversation leading into, maybe, a date at the end of it. Now it had gone from sharing pleasantries and in only a matter of seconds, turned into World War Three. She pressed herself back into her pillow and winced. Her head was still sore. Killian felt awful.

'Wow, wow, wow, I'm sorry,' Killian repeated with hands raised. 'Penny, Penny, I only meant that Cleo and I are just colleagues. And I'm sorry if I upset you. I honestly didn't mean to. I'm not good at these things,' he admitted. 'Look, let's calm down and start again. Cleo is gay — a lesbian — and wouldn't want me if I were the last person on earth. And, and, I don't want her either,' he quickly added. 'In fact...' He took a breath. 'If I'm honest with myself, I want to spend some time with... you,' he said and stopped talking. Penny's distraught face turned slowly to a smile. 'But she is beautiful,' Killian quickly added and got a grape tossed at his face for his cheek. 'Stop it,' Killian responded and picked the grape up off the bed and swallowed it in one.

'Serves your right,' Penny said smugly, her blue eyes glistening.

'Anyway, Relic,' Killian got to the point.

'So my poor milkman turned into Relic?' Penny's eyes widened when she remembered him grabbing her on her doorstep.

'Yes, I'm afraid so,' Killian responded.

'He has a wife,' she said solemnly.

'Does he? That's awful.' Killian felt sad for his

family.

'Where is Relic now?' Penny asked.

'I sent him back. He won't be bothering us again.' He looked certain.

'Can he come back here? Are you sure?' Penny argued, still scared.

'No. I sent him back with a permanent spell. He can never return to this world,' Killian said with confidence.

'So that's it? Everything is back to normal?' Penny sighed.

'Things are never back to normal in the spirit world, Penny. It'll be only a matter of time before something else turns up.'

'Well, talking of that, Hathaway has expressed that he wants to keep you on the payroll. He wants us to work together when a case rears its ugly head,' Penny told him.

'Well, that's good news,' Killian agreed.

'So, how about a proper date when I get out of here?' Penny said with confidence.

'Wow, you don't mess about do you?' Killian responded. 'Yep, I'm up for that. I have to go now and deal with something else, but tell me when and where and I'll be there.'

'Okay. Thursday night at seven in the Square Inn?' Penny suggested.

Killian giggled and looked deep into her eyes. She bit her bottom lip and he leaned in to give her a peck on the cheek. But she grabbed him in a full-on suck-face kiss, which almost pulled him onto the bed. When they eventually broke away, he could feel his excitement building and needed to go and cool down somewhere. 'There's more where that came from,' she chuckled.

'I'll see you on Thursday. I'll pick you up and we can walk there together,' he said and made his way out of the hospital and back to his apartment.

Chapter 19
The Box

The weather was beautiful and later that morning Killian decided he would walk to Zoot's house and pick up his scooter, rather than catch a bus. It took him an hour or so to finally get there. The heat was immense and Killian forgot to take water with him. He licked his dry lips and felt a comfortable feeling inside when he saw Zoot's house. He could see the bike parked out the front, with his blue helmet on the seat. He approached the building and stepped up onto the porch.

The door was partially open so Killian gave it a quick knock and stepped inside.

'Zoot. Zoot. It's Killian,' he called out.

'I'm here. Outside in the garden.' He heard Zoot's muffled tones from beyond the passageway. The house was as pristine as usual and the wizard made his way through to the garden. Sure enough, his friend was sitting on a large, white, comfortable-looking sofa. There was a canopy tied to a wooden frame, which kept the occupier in the shade.

'Come, sit, my friend,' Zoot said patting the

cushion.

'Cleo got you home safe and sound then?' Killian said.

'Yes. Where did you find her? She's terrific,' Zoot said, sounding impressed. 'She's such a great ally and we couldn't have done any of this without her.'

'Somehow I don't think it'll be the last we see of her, my friend,' Killian said smiling.

'I hope not. She's lovely,' Zoot added.

'Anyway.' Killian broke away from the subject matter, not wanting to disappoint Zoot if he had any romantic thoughts towards her. 'You are looking great, my friend,' Killian gushed. 'You were a complete wreck yesterday.' Zoot's lacerations and contusions were completely cleared up. 'Is the rest of your body healed also?' Killian questioned.

'Yes, everything is repaired, but it does take time for the body to heal itself. It doesn't just happen overnight. It will take a few days for everything to heal properly,' Zoot clarified.

'You'll have to tell me your secret,' Killian joked and looked at him.

'Well, you know what it is,' Zoot added. 'There's no big secret to the immortal.'

'I know it's to do with the box, Zoot, but what exactly does it do?' Killian was curious to find out the process the monk used.

'All I do is remove the stone from the box and place it next to me and sit,' he said.

'What? And that's it?' Killian pressed.

'There is a bit more to it than that. You also have to believe and meditate,' Zoot explained.

'Well, I'm happy that you're in a better place, my friend,' Killian said truthfully.

'You look troubled, my friend.' Zoot noticed a look of uncertainty in Killian's eyes. Killian took a deep breath and closed his eyes. He opened them again and Zoot knew there was a big question coming.

'It's just that. Relic, well…' he said.

'What about Relic?' Zoot responded, leaning in.

'I need to know how it crossed over in the first place,' Killian said and pursed his lips.

'I think I know,' Zoot spoke up, 'but I would like to offer you a glass of cloudy lemonade first,' he said. He could see how hot his friend appeared.

Killian wanted him to carry on right away and tell him his idea. But he knew whatever Zoot was going to say would have to wait. You never refused Zoot's hospitality, or he would get really offended. Besides, Killian loved his homemade lemonade and at that moment, with the hot weather, he would have killed for a cool drink. The monk disappeared into the house and soon returned with a tray. He had a couple of glasses and a big, jug filled to the brim with ice and lemon slices floating on top of the misty liquid.

Once he'd poured two glasses and they took a drink each, he spoke.

'There was a bad storm a few days ago,' Zoot remembered.

'Yeah,' Killian recalled, 'and after that, the weather broke and we got this lovely sunshine,' Killian cut in. 'Sorry, Zoot,' the warlock apologised. He knew Zoot hated to be interrupted.

'I believe that storm caused a big electrical surge in the atmosphere, which left a weakness between our world and the dark world,' Zoot said knowingly. Killian looked at him and stroked his chin in thought.

Suddenly, like a light being switched on in his head, Killian brightened up and then grimaced. 'The pub,' Killian realised.

Zoot nodded.

'The Square Inn used to be a temple for the worship of evil thousands of years ago. The Druids used to hold their ceremonies on that very ground where the car park is now. That's why it appeared there and attacked Toady in that very spot. And why it all happened in the first place. There must still be some kind of energy there and I have to seal it so that it can't happen again.' Killian was up on his feet now and almost ranting.

'Hold it there, Killian. It isn't your fault,' Zoot

sympathised with his friend.

'But I should have realised when I first moved here,' Killian hissed. 'It's my local, for fuck's sake. Er, sorry, Zoot, for swearing, mate,' Killian apologised.

'Don't worry, but don't do it again,' he said with a straight face and then warmed up with a grin. 'It's as much my fault as yours.'

'How's it yours?' Killian poked for an answer. 'You're not a warlock—no offence,' Killian said.

'None taken,' Zoot responded and sipped a little more lemonade. 'I have perception and my senses didn't tell me anything,' he said begrudgingly, 'and I've lived here longer than you.'

Killian looked at his piercing deep, brown eyes and gave in. 'I should have felt it, you should have felt it… it doesn't matter. I've got to seal it once and for all and hope that nothing else has come through in the meantime,' Killian said with a shudder. 'I'll do it tonight when everyone is asleep, otherwise, it will look really suspicious. And I don't want to be explaining anything to the police at this point. I've wasted too much time at that station already.'

'How's the lovely Penny?' Zoot asked.

'How do you…? Oh, never mind,' Killian said, not wanting to question his friend who knew everything about everybody. 'She's fine. In fact,

I've got a date with her on Thursday,' he confessed.

'She's lovely. You're a lucky guy... and Killian,' Zoot uttered, just before he left for home.

'Yes, Zoot,' Killian knew there was something else coming.

'Don't mess it up,' he added with a grin. Killian smiled and they hugged one another.

'Thanks for everything, Zoot,' Killian said sincerely.

'I'm always here when you need my help,' Zoot said, 'by the way...'

'Yeah?' Killian turned back on his way to his bike.

'I'm curious. How did Chief Inspector Hathaway explain all this to the press?' Zoot was really interested to know. He never normally took too much interest in the local news unless it was important.

'His press officer made up a story of some kind of wild animal on the loose from a wildlife park. Which has been found and dealt with apparently. The other stuff, Toady went mad after drinking too much.' Killian shrugged his shoulders. 'We will always know what happened though.' He waved goodbye to Zoot and was gone.

That night Killian made his way to the Square Inn car park and sat on the cool ground. He cast a spell that would hopefully seal his world forever from the evils of the dark places.

Chapter 20
The Date

The week was uneventful with nothing coming in — in the way of work. It was lucky he'd received the payment from Chief Hathaway, which kept the wolves from the door. Penny was eventually discharged from hospital and soon she was well enough to spend an evening out. Thursday came along and so Killian changed their plans and invited her over to his place for a meal. At seven that evening there was a knock on his door and he let her in. Penny wore a long blue summer dress with a low neckline and a split halfway up her thigh. She wore her hair piled up on top with ringlets, which hung down each side of her beautiful face.

'Hi, Penny,' Killian said in welcome, 'how are you feeling?' She didn't have to answer because she looked amazing.

'I'm fine, honestly. It was nice to change out of pyjama's and back into normal clothes,' she said and the old sparkle was there in her eyes. 'My head is totally good now.' He couldn't see the last of the bruising as she'd cleverly covered that up with make-up.

'Come on in.' Killian gestured for her to walk through and he led her to his living room. 'Please, take a seat. Would you like a drink, Wine?'

'I try not to,' she said.

'Wow, Penny White coming out with a joke. That's new.' Killian laughed.

'Watch it, Mr Spooks,' she said. 'White wine, please. I am trying to be more relaxed since the... accident.' It was still raw, even Killian could see that.

'Prosecco,' Killian said.

'Yes, please. You remembered, wow — I'm officially impressed,' she gushed, her eyes bright. Killian didn't normally keep much in the way of alcohol in his apartment besides whisky. But on this occasion he'd made the effort of buying a couple of bottles.

'Something smells — ' she was about to say.

'Good... I hope,' Killian cut in, 'please say good,' he repeated. She laughed and her whole face lit up. 'It's just spaghetti Bolognese,' he said.

'Yeah, I was about to say it smells good. Don't worry — well, until I've tasted it,' she joked.

'You sure you're okay?' Killian probed. 'You took a really hard knock.'

'Honestly, I'm fine. Has anything happened since that day?' Penny asked as Killian handed her a wine glass.

'No talking shop tonight, just nice food, great wine and lovely company,' Killian reminded her.

'Okay,' she agreed with a gentle nod. They sat and ate and the evening was rolling along with pleasant conversation and they didn't even notice the time. They sat on the sofa; the low lighting from a few candles littered over the room and made for a romantic setting. Killian looked at her through dreamy eyes. God, she was beautiful.

'Whisky,' he announced, trying to bring himself out of it.

'You trying to get me drunk and have your wicked way with me, Mr Spooks?' Penny teased. He didn't answer and got up from the sofa and brought back two, large glasses. They both took a sip and the warmth of the liquor loosened any inhibitions.

'It's getting late,' Penny said and as she looked into his eyes, there was a wickedness that taunted him.

'Do you want me to call you an Uber?' Killian asked softly as they slowly pulled together on the sofa.

'But my name is Penny,' she responded seriously, and Killian gave her a look of confusion. And she burst out laughing. And then Killian got the joke — closed his eyes and shook his head.

'You did another joke, Penny. Did someone buy you a joke book in hospital, so you could come out with the worst ones for our date?' he responded. 'Is that why you came here tonight?'

'Yes, exactly, crazy right?' she said, her eyes glossing over, her lips inviting and rosy. He breathed in her perfume, which was more intoxicating than the wine. She spoke in a low, smooth, sexy tone. 'It's like I'm really interesting to be with right?'

'Definitely —'

But before he could say anything else, she leaned forward and pressed her lips against his. They were soon locked in a long, lingering and passionate embrace. She darted her tongue into his mouth and toyed with his. She ran her fingers through his hair and traced a line across his neck. Soon they were rolling about on the sofa in a heated tangle. She began unbuttoning his shirt, while he was pulling at the zipper of her dress. It didn't take long for them to get naked and make their way to his bedroom. The sound of smacking lips and panting breath filled the air. They didn't speak, just intertwined in each other's arms. The lovers fell on the bed, gently clawing at one another in a passionate frenzy. He could feel the peaks of her breasts brush against his naked chest. She pushed herself against him, caressing and toying, licking and devouring. He traced a finger down her smooth body and felt the soft, moistness of her inner thigh... and then nothing else mattered. The taxi wasn't needed.

Penny woke to the aroma of coffee and bright sunlight, which poured in through the window. The bedroom door was open and she called out to him.

'So does this mean that we're boyfriend and girlfriend now?' she asked. Killian sighed as he came in and sat on the bed.

'I guess it does, Miss White,' he said and with that he got a smack in the face with a pillow. 'Sorry, Penny.' He smiled. Soon it was time for her to go and Killian called a taxi.

'I'm back in work on Monday,' she told him.

'So I guess we'll still be working together?' he added.

'Yes, I guess so. It'll be weird though,' she said.

'Not really — I mean what's so weird about a girl who's in a close relationship with a wizard,' Killian mused.

'Close eh?' she teased and they kissed again before she left. 'I'll do dinner next time.' And with that she was gone.

What will the next case be, he pondered?

THE END

Printed in Great Britain
by Amazon